"We could see each other for dinner."

Avery frowned, shifting the chart in her hands. "Maybe socializing isn't such a good idea with me being your physical therapist."

"Why not? Because you said everything outside of the office was fair game."

Her face flushed. "That's not what I meant and you know it."

His male instincts urged him to stalk closer, crowd her in and make her admit she was just as attracted as he was. Instead he forced himself to remain still, using words to reel her in. "Come on. You want an adventure. I want to help you find one. Let's talk about it over dinner."

"Well..." Her flush deepened, but she also straightened her shoulders. "I guess I could do dinner one night."

As he came to his feet, Avery's quizzical little smile distracted him. He saw nothing else. Not taupe walls, nor yellow scrubs. Just pale blue eyes and bow-shaped lips as she moved closer.

Before he could reach for his cane, his legs gave him the old heave-ho and collapsed. Avery had moved close, too close to miss out on his game of timber. Down they both went.

"Sweetheart, you're the softest landing place I've had in a while."

* * *

The Renegade Returns is part of the Mill Town Millionaires series from Dani Wade.

Dear Reader,

Fast cars, family versus career, reputation building and breaking, and a tragic accident that changes lives in an instant...Luke Blackstone, brother number three in the Mill Town Millionaires series, packed a lot of action into his book. But his heroine, Avery Prescott, knew their tale, at its core, was a love story that started when they were teenagers. Getting these two strong people to find middle ground was a challenge, but when they did, I found it oh so magical.

I'd love to hear what y'all think of Luke and Avery's reunion romance! You can email me at readdaniwade@gmail.com or follow me on Facebook. As always, news about my releases is easiest to find through my author newsletter, which you can sign up for on my website, daniwade.com.

Enjoy!

Dani

DANI WADE

THE RENEGADE RETURNS

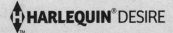

Recycling programs
for this product may
not exist in your area

ISBN-13: 978-0-373-73473-3

The Renegade Returns

www.Harlequin.com

Printed in U.S.A.

Dani Wade astonished her local librarians as a teenager when she carried home ten books every week—and actually read them all. Now she writes her own characters, who clamor for attention in the midst of the chaos that is her life. Residing in the Southern United States with a husband, two kids, two dogs and one grumpy cat, she stays busy until she can closet herself away with her characters once more.

Books by Dani Wade

Harlequin Desire

His by Design

Mill Town Millionaires

A Bride's Tangled Vows
The Blackstone Heir
The Renegade Returns

Visit the Author Profile page at Harlequin.com, or daniwade.com, for more titles.

To My Mother

You instilled an early love of reading in me that has shaped who I truly am. Your encouragement throughout my life has helped me believe in myself, even when it was hard. Every day I use the dedicated work ethic and practicality you taught me to make my dreams a reality. Thank you.

I've watched up close as you've fought hard, worked steadfastly, prayed with belief and loved with everything in you. I only hope someday to be able to do the same half as well as you. All my love...

One

Ignoring stares and whispers was an art form Lucas Blackstone had perfected. The more wins he claimed as a stock car racer, the more attention he attracted. Which was normally fine by him. In fact, he thrived on it.

Used to thrive on it.

Tonight, he wished he could fade into the wainscoting on the walls so people would stop staring. Stop whispering about his arrival at the country club. Stop measuring the difficulty with which he walked to his family's chosen table. Stop speculating about whether his racing days as Renegade Blackstone were permanently over.

Just as he did during the long, dark hours of every night.

Instead, he pretended this was a normal night, a

normal dinner with his family. Not his debut before his hometown after having his body broken into more pieces than any man should experience.

His back straight, he vowed to himself that he would beat this with every single step.

"You're doing so well," Christina softly encouraged him as he carefully placed each footfall on the way to their table. As their resident nurse and his brother Aiden's wife, she had been tracking Luke's progress since his accident earlier this year. "But by the end of the evening, you might be wishing for that wheelchair you refused."

"No," he said through teeth he tried not to clench. He didn't quite succeed.

He would not resort to invalid status. The marble-handled cane he leaned on was his single concession to his still-healing legs. The *plonk* every time it met the floor sounded loud in his head, even though he knew it hardly made a sound.

"All that macho stoicism will lead to one thing," she warned as they reached their destination. Then she rolled her eyes when the men all booed. "I'm serious, Luke. Pretending you don't need help will just make getting out of bed tomorrow more painful."

"You're so cute when you're concerned," he cooed back, laughing when she stuck out her tongue.

The reality couldn't always be covered by his teasing mask—but he sure tried. He'd become a close buddy with pain since his car accident. During everyday tasks, during rehabilitation. Sometimes it shot through him under the cloak of a dead sleep. He hated it, but pain could be good. The sharp sting reminded him he was alive. Not just a shell, a body that would never feel again.

Luke lived for high speeds. Recovery at a snail's pace could only be described as pure torture. Some days, he'd give anything to take his mind off his present state.

"You keep babying him, and he'll wish he'd never consented to coming home," Aiden teased his bride.

All the attention aside, Luke knew being back in Black Hills would be good for him. Helping his brothers out at the mill that supported the entire town would surely blunt the aching need to return to his race car. After a year of what they all suspected was sabotage to their business by an inside source, the family needed all hands on deck.

This is only temporary...

To his relief, he managed to seat himself after only a minor skirmish with the long tablecloth. *Damn accoutrements.* But the formal atmosphere had been the deciding factor in choosing to eat here tonight. Hope against hope it might keep nosy, small-town people in their seats—for a while.

"Stop pulling at your collar, Luke," his twin brother, Jacob, reprimanded.

But Luke couldn't help it. He was as ill at ease as his brother was comfortable in a suit. Even now his hand crept back up to tug at the tie around his neck— give him a racing suit any day. "This damn thing is almost as uncomfortable as all the people staring," he grumped. His comfort zone had always been his car—not polished silver, gold-rimmed china and fresh flower centerpieces.

"Well, most of these people are family friends, but

they still love a celebrity. They can't help the need to watch," Aiden explained in his tolerant older-brother voice.

"I just enjoyed it more when they were in awe of my good looks." *Instead of speculating about my doom.*

Luke's teasing tone left his brothers and the women laughing, and gratitude added another layer to his self-defense. The maudlin martyr was not his most sought-after role. Only he knew there was a kernel of truth in his humor, and he would keep it that way. So he covered his discomfort as carefully as he draped his cloth napkin over his lap.

After ordering, Luke deemed it safe to let his gaze skim the softly lit room. A lot of faces had aged since he'd been in high school, though they were still familiar. It had been many years since he'd left town to start an incredibly successful racing career but he'd returned for a few events. Some fund-raisers. Anything to make his visits home more bearable. He had spent time with his incapacitated mother and Christina, who was her nurse. After that, his only thought had been getting himself out of the house without running into his domineering grandfather.

Escape. If his life had a theme song, that would be the refrain. Now that the old man had kicked the bucket, Blackstone Manor had transformed into a home—thanks to the people around this table.

About halfway across the crowded space Luke's gaze snagged on a tawny, upswept head of hair. The woman's profile was sharper than it had been in high school, more refined. Gone was the softness of a young woman, now honed into a sphinxlike silhouette that immediately captured his eye.

Avery Prescott. Now that he thought about it, he hadn't seen her on any of his visits home. Which was odd—and from the looks of her, a total shame.

As if feeling his gaze, she glanced his way with pale blue eyes. Despite the distance between them, something jolted through his body. Deeper than an *I know you*, but not a lightning flash. More a wash of awareness that flooded over all his uncomfortable emotions, muting them to radio silence. When she quickly turned back to her dining companions, he had an urge to stand, to command her attention.

This was a pleasant surprise. Luke had always enjoyed women—the sight, sound and smell of them—but there'd been nothing since his accident. Not even when surrounded by a hospital floor full of pretty nurses. Oh, he'd flirt and play, but it had covered a storm of pain, worry and frustration that he didn't know how to calm now that his one mode of escape had been snatched from him.

But tonight, watching Avery as she smiled and conversed with her dinner companions sent an electric spark of attraction tingling down his spine. Her frequent glances in his direction made him wonder if she felt it, too, but their eyes never met again.

Avoiding him, huh?

Throughout dinner and conversing with a few brave visitors, his awareness remained. Finally she stood to leave, giving him his first unhindered look at her slender figure. Her sheath dress showcased curves right where he liked them, proportionate to her delicate bone structure.

She made her way through the tables with elegant grace, pausing to smile and speak to several people, but never for long. The candlelight from the center-pieces reflected off her earrings, lending sparkle to her slight glow. Her black sequined dress reminded him of her family's wealth and the undeniable fact that she belonged in this place. Still she refused to look his way.

He thought she was going to avoid their table al-together, until Christina stood to wave. "Avery, over here," she called.

Avery's hesitation was noticeable, at least to Luke. But then again, he'd barely taken his eyes off her to look at his plate. Why didn't she want to stop and say hi?

His memories were of a gawky girl, shy, always on the fringes. Under direct attention, she would stum-ble over her words, drop things, trip over her own feet. Tonight she moved with a type of deliberate grace. Head high. Steps secure. This new Avery fas-cinated him.

Her greeting included them all, when a need inside Luke wanted her to rest those pale blue eyes on him. He kept his body on lockdown, refusing to draw her attention until it was freely given.

"Having dinner with Doc Morris again, I see?" Aiden said with a grin.

"If his wife wasn't with us, some rumors might have started by now."

Luke soaked in the slight movements of her hands, the shrug of those delicate shoulders as everyone chatted around him. *This is crazy—the last thing you need is to get involved with someone here. You're re-*

covering. Still he couldn't look away, couldn't ignore the draw he felt growing deep inside.

"Doc says someone has to make sure I'm eating. We don't want to lose a community asset after he worked so hard to get me into good schools and internships," she added in a decent replication of the older man.

As a round of chuckles rose from the table, she finally glanced his way—and those sparks inside him multiplied. "Um, hi, Luke." With that slight stall, the first small chink in her sophisticated armor appeared.

He remembered those same words spoken to him with the enthusiasm of a young girl trying hard to hide her crush, but not quite succeeding. Now, that awkward innocence had morphed into a sophisticated woman with a restrained politeness, as if by keeping herself under tight control she could prevent a repeat of the embarrassments of her youth.

Somehow, he didn't like this as much as his memories.

"Are you a doctor now?" Luke asked. How could he have been home so often and never thought to ask what had happened to the young girl who had hung around the edges of their social circle?

Her gaze touched on his before skittering away. "Actually, I'm a physical therapist."

Ouch. His recent painful visits for therapy did not make that a happy revelation. Very unexpected. Very unwelcome.

"In fact," Aiden said with an amused tone that set Luke's nerves on edge, "she's *your* physical therapist."

In a flash, Luke relived the agony of his therapy sessions over the last three months and winced. Pain forced things to the surface, compelled a man to reveal way more emotion than he wanted other people to see. "Oh, hell no," he muttered.

Apparently his words weren't low enough, because Avery's elegant features took on a hint of frost. "I'm afraid you don't have a choice. I'm the only physical therapist in Black Hills. Or within fifty miles of it."

Damn. "I didn't mean…"

Her body straightened, gaining only a slight inch in stature. "And I'm a damn good one, too."

"Everyone around here knows that."

Luke had been so focused on Avery that he hadn't noticed the approach of anyone else. Next to her now stood Mark Zabinski, an old high school friend of Jacob's and part of the upper management at Blackstone Mills.

"So the Renegade is back," Mark went on, ignoring Luke's lack of welcome. "And causing quite the stir."

"That I am." Might as well own it.

Avery glanced around the table, surveying the reunited Blackstone family. Her voice was hushed compared to Mark's forceful tone. "It must be strange, having all of you back here, together again."

Very few people would notice the phenomenon, much less mention how each brother had left, then returned to find their place in Black Hills now that their grandfather was dead. But this was Avery. He remembered glimpses of her standing on the edge of the crowd in high school, alone but not missing an ounce of what occurred.

Aiden's dark gaze swept over them all before he smiled. "Yes, but family is good. Very good."

Luke wouldn't have gotten through the last few

months without family, including both his brothers, Christina and Jacob's fiancé, KC. "Amen," he agreed.

But as the conversation continued around them, Luke didn't miss the dark shadow that clouded Avery's eyes, the subtle shift of her expression. And he certainly didn't miss Mark's hand casually lying against the small of her back. A sign of ownership, possessiveness, protection. Comfort for a friend? Or something more?

Avery didn't move away, but she also didn't relax into the touch, either. *Interesting.*

"Mark," Jacob said, his tone firming to one of authority, "I'm glad you stopped by. The computer gurus are finally coming to install the new computer system at the plant. Time for an upgrade like we talked about last month," Jacob continued. "We'll meet early tomorrow morning to discuss it."

Mark shifted on his feet, his dress shoes squeaking under the stress. "Great."

Mark smiled as he said it, but Luke suspected he wasn't as thrilled as he tried to look. Something about the overstretch of his smile, giving his face a slightly Joker edge.

"Avery, let me escort you to the valet," Mark said, using that damnable hand to steer her away. She nodded, her gaze making a warm sweep of the table… while studiously avoiding Luke.

Why did that leave him feeling cold?

Escorting a woman—something Luke couldn't do with ease anymore. As if she knew his thoughts followed them, Avery glanced back over her shoulder, but a cool mask still protected her emotions.

Great. Just what he needed—a ticked-off physical

therapist with the ability to visit pain on him with a simple twitch of her wrist. His dismissal of her abilities had given her motivation aplenty for inflicting a twinge or two on him.

But Luke was used to using his charm to get out of sticky situations—turning them into something positive, something entertaining. Despite the complication, his curiosity grew. So did his unexpected need. He'd been lost in a miasma of pain and frustration that seriously weighed him down. But this kick-start to his motor had lifted him up, exhilarated him. A relationship was nowhere on his agenda, but a little battle of wills would definitely liven up his current dull existence.

A few fireworks to dull the pain. What could be more fun than that?

How could anyone look so cute in scrubs? Not that Avery was the type to appreciate being categorized as *cute*. She probably preferred *capable*. Her sunny yellow scrubs were paired with a no-nonsense expression and friendly, but impersonal, tone. Her detachment caused him to itch after the receptionist brought him through the double doors into the heart of the therapy facility.

If Avery thought her all-business attitude would keep him at arm's length, she'd get a surprise. He'd just tease his way through whatever crack he could find in her armor. The challenge brought a surge of energy. Besides, befriending her might keep her from taking any vengeance out on his bones.

An impressive workout room occupied an open central space in the main part of the building. Top-of-the-line equipment gleamed from careful upkeep. Avery gestured him through a side door and closed them inside. The treatment room had the same look of quality, including a padded table, small desk and comfortable chairs. "This place is really nice. You've done well for yourself, Avery," he said.

The compliment garnered him his first genuine smile. No pretense. "Thank you. This building has been a blessing to me and to my patients."

And it obviously meant a lot to her. "You named the clinic after your mother."

"Yes." Her smile dimmed a little, awakening an urge to give her a comforting hug just as he would Christina, who'd proven to be a true friend.

Avery continued. "We became exceptionally close during her illness. Besides, she provided the funding for a bigger, better clinic for the community in my inheritance. We're very lucky to have it."

Her pride in her accomplishment added a glow to her expression, awakening jealousy in Luke's gut. He remembered being proud of what he did, but the memories were fading from sharp to hazy, obscured by the turmoil of recent months.

This woman used her healing talents every day in a community that needed her. How fulfilling must that be? "You have plenty of patients?"

She nodded, sending her thick ponytail swinging. "I like to think it's because I do good work, and not just because I'm the only convenient choice."

"I bet it is. You must be good with your hands, huh?"

To his surprise, that professional demeanor slipped and she fumbled the chart from her hands. It hit the ground with a clatter. "That's really inappropriate, Luke," she warned with a frown.

He hadn't meant it to be, but now that he thought about it that way... He watched as a flush of pink swept up her neck and into her cheeks. Oh, she could be proper all she wanted, but now he knew—she might've grown up, but this chickadee was still as easily flustered as she'd been in high school.

Teasing her was gonna be entertaining. And her all-business attitude screamed for him to bring a little fun, a little laughter into her life. Since he could use some fun, too, he'd be doing them both a favor. Right?

"I'm pretty well known for saying whatever comes to mind," he said with a grin. "And being handsome. And charming." It wasn't bragging, 'cause it was true.

"And obnoxiously self-absorbed?" The contrast between her words and sickly sweet tone made him laugh. A true laugh. Man, that felt good.

He conceded with a sexy grin. "Maybe. Occasionally."

That professional mask slipped a fraction more before she smoothed her palms over already sleek hair, back to her ponytail.

He was getting somewhere now. Just a little more ribbing, and she might actually laugh like a real person instead of a robot.

She pulled out a rolling stool and sat, propping his folder on her lap. Guess it was down-to-business time, which wasn't nearly as amusing. Luke had worked hard at recovery, but this was the first time fun had appeared anywhere in his current nightmare. He didn't want to leave it behind.

"Goals?" she asked, focusing her attention on the papers.

That was easy enough. His one goal had been blazing in his brain since the accident. "To be back in my car. ASAP."

Avery glanced up, those gorgeous eyes wide, drawing him in. "That's pretty decisive."

"You say that like it's a bad thing." Her tone left him defensive, when there was no need for it. Then again, Luke's life had been spent on goals other people just didn't get. "You asked. I answered."

Her frown and longer-than-polite stare awakened an urge to squirm he hadn't encountered since third grade.

"Most of my patients are more worried about walking unaided again," she mused, as if talking to herself rather than him.

Alarm streaked along his nerves. He didn't want her thinking too hard, digging too deep. So he grinned. "Oh, I have other goals."

After a minute of silence, she made a speed-up gesture with the pen in her hand. "And..."

"Having a good time doesn't sound nearly as professional, if you know what I mean."

The pen hit the floor. Instant color stained her creamy cheeks. Wow. When was the last time he'd seen a blush like that? It must have been— A memory burst inside his brain. *High school.*

"Do you need some help with that?"

The jolt that rushed through him had to be from surprise. After all, who would have expected Little Miss Perfect to offer to help him change clothes? A blush spread over her rounded cheeks to match the heat racing over his body.

He looked from the dry shorts in his hand back to Avery in the first bikini he'd ever seen her wear. Must have been bought special for this final summer bash for seniors at the lake before everyone flew off to the colleges of their choice. Everyone except him—his destination was North Carolina and any racing track they'd let him drive on. But even the prospect of finally leaving home hadn't made him reckless enough to initiate the greenest girl in their group. No matter what her pale blue eyes were begging for. "Honey, helping me would involve a lot more than a change of clothes."

"I know." But that flush on her fair skin, bright enough to see in the dim light this far from the bonfire, told him she didn't truly know what she was offering.

To his surprise, a shot of adrenaline flashed through his veins. The same kind that came with hundred-mile-an-hour speeds and the feel of the wheel beneath his palms. Not the sexy slide into arousal he usually got with girls. Even his alcohol-soaked brain knew this was a bad idea, despite his body's approval. Better to stop this before it began, even if it meant being harsh…

"I think somebody with more experience would be a bigger help to me."

Oh, no. How could Luke have forgotten that long-ago summer night? Without thought, he said, "Holy— Avery, I can't believe you came on to me that night."

The little rolling stool shot backward, as far across

the tiny exam room as she could go. The thump as she hit the opposite wall went unnoticed by her. She only stared, her flush deepening, spreading down her neck and chest to disappear under the yellow scrubs. "I—"

Why had he said that? Whatever he thought usually slid out of his mouth without any semblance of a stop sign in between, that's why. Most people found it funny. But her utter mortification was not what he'd wanted.

"I'm sorry, Avery. I should never have said that." His mama had taught him to own up to his mistakes. People might think he was all ego—and he let them keep believing it—but he'd never dishonor a woman or ignore her distress. "Seriously, I may not always play the gentleman, but I would never intentionally embarrass a friend."

Her recovery was quick. She straightened on the stool and crept forward with her heels until she'd crossed half the little room. He couldn't help but notice she still kept some distance between them. The return of the professional mask took a little longer, though. "Friends, huh?"

He grinned, hoping to put her at ease. "I'd like to think so."

She nodded, as if that settled things. But it took her a few moments to say, "So I wanted a little walk on the wild side." She shrugged those delicately built shoulders, keeping her eyes trained on his chart. "What high school senior doesn't?"

His libido urged him to ask if she'd gotten it, but for once he kept his trap shut. He sifted through his memories for any gossip he'd heard about her, but came up empty. All Jacob had supplied last night were the directions to the therapy center. No bad behavior. No scandalous liaisons.

Was there no gossip to be had? Last night she'd been at dinner with Doctor Morris and his wife, who were seventy if they were a day. She'd had no date accompanying her, even though Mark had joined her to walk out. No wedding ring on her long, slender fingers. Her last name hadn't changed. Maybe there hadn't been any wild times...

Maybe he should change that?

Oh. Hell. No. The last thing he needed was a casual hookup with the least casual woman he knew. He tried to erase the seductive thought as she spoke again.

"We'll start each session with a warm-up, then build strength with resistance exercises—first using just your body weight, then moving up," she was saying, using her pen to check off her points. Her precision marks were a little too perfect, holding her interest a little too much. "Your therapist in North Carolina gave me your records. You've come an incredibly long way, but today I'd like to see what's happening for myself..."

Luke didn't want to think about any of it—so he distracted himself with the fall of soft yellow scrubs that skimmed her curves. If she knew what he was thinking right now, she'd probably give him an exaggerated frown and tell him that activity wasn't on his approved list.

Maybe he'd have to prove her wrong.

"Okay, Luke?"

"Yep," he automatically answered.

"You weren't listening, were you?"

"Nope."

The look on her face implied he'd been naughty, but it was her big sigh, the one that lifted her nicely rounded breasts, that drew his attention. Not the sigh, just the— Boy, he was in *so* much trouble.

"I guess I'll explain as we go along," she said, ignoring his distraction. She rose to her feet and turned to open the door. "Let's see what you're capable of..."

That didn't sound good, and his previous experience with physical therapy told Luke it wouldn't be. She started him on a slow walk around the room, moving alongside him. Her soothing voice washed over him, almost relaxing despite the awkward coordination of his uncooperative legs and the cane.

Except he knew what was coming.

The upper body work wasn't an issue. Moving and challenging those muscles actually felt good. His hips and legs—not so much. Avery put him through some resistance training, range-of-motion work and stretching. An hour later, drenched in sweat, he had to wonder if a sadistic grin lurked behind her ardent expression. Her encouraging words said she wanted to help, but was she secretly satisfied by his pain?

After all, he'd humiliated her in high school. That he'd done it for her own good didn't seem like adequate justification now that he was an adult. But maybe he could make it up to her somehow?

Or would spending time with Avery outside of his therapy be the equivalent of playing with fire?

Two

Avery ignored the shake of her hands as she removed electrode pads from Luke's legs and lower back. Thank goodness she didn't have to do anything complicated. Otherwise she'd surely have made an idiot of herself. The sight of his body in nothing but athletic shorts was a test to her professionalism.

She cleared her throat, trying to ease the constriction. "I'll let you get dressed and then meet you up front."

Except thoughts of Luke and clothes only reminded her of their earlier conversation, and her immature offer to help him dress. *Ah, there are those stomach-twisting nerves again.* She hurried out the door with only a small bump against the frame.

Luke was so much like she remembered—only ten times more dangerous. Obviously, he'd figured out that these joking innuendos were the way to get beneath her guard. She needed a way to counteract them.

Her current method wasn't working very well.

Teasing from any man under sixty flustered her, but her reactions to Luke were too strong—a tempest compared to a sprinkle of rain when it came to other men. The fact that she found him amazingly attractive only made her nerves worse. Her interest had nothing to do with him being a local celebrity and everything to do with him being, well, Luke.

His charm and ready smile had drawn her from the moment she'd met him. Whenever they'd seen each other as teenagers at country club dinners or various gatherings, Avery would follow him around, subtly watching him. Unlike his brother Jacob, who had surrounded himself with a businesslike wall, Luke knew how to make himself comfortable in any social situation.

A skill Avery had never developed.

Oh, she could chat with people in town, people she'd known all her life. Her genuine interest in and sympathy for her patients made interacting with them easy. And she had a few girlfriends, like Christina, whom she could turn to when she really needed to talk.

But drop her into a bunch of strangers and Avery simply froze. She reverted back to her high school speech class, with all those eyes staring at her, waiting for her to say something brilliant—and all she could do was squeak.

"So how often do I need to be here?"

As Luke approached, Avery looked up from the

chart she wasn't really reading. Even with the cane, she could have sworn a sexy male model had invaded her territory. Her breath caught in her throat once more, before she released it on a sigh.

Who was she kidding? She'd tried to ride that train once, and Luke had made it plain she wasn't his type. If he never brought that night up again, it would be too soon. Besides, Luke wouldn't be sticking around for long. He'd made that perfectly plain during their discussion.

Why risk more humiliation by reading into his teasing more than he could possibly mean? She knew from countless hours of observation that, for Luke, flirting was a way of life.

She forced herself to erase any mooning, wistful tendencies from her voice. She kept it short and, okay, maybe a little stiff. "Let's get you set up for Wednesday, shall we? I won't have an exact plan until I've looked over my notes from today."

Avery's receptionist was flirtier than usual, giving Luke a run for his money. Cindy had all the outgoing personality that had passed Avery by. She chatted and giggled with Luke as she scheduled his next appointment. Normally Avery appreciated that Cindy made their patients smile, but today their laughter left her feeling like an outsider—though she'd never admit that to anyone.

"And what's this?"

Avery barely quelled the instinctive grab for what she didn't want him to see. She narrowed her eyes at Cindy. They'd been looking at the brochure earlier and Avery was pretty sure she'd asked Cindy to put it away. Yet there it was, sitting on the checkout counter, as pretty as you please.

"Cindy..." Avery warned. That innocent expression didn't fool Avery.

She tried a glare, but Cindy just laughed it off. "Rock climbing and rappelling—not far from here," the receptionist said. "Can you believe it? Avery's been on a search for 'adventure' lately." The air quotes didn't help Avery feel better.

"Really?"

Luke's drawl should not send shivers down her spine. And his slow perusal over her body should not make her mouth water. As if satisfied with what he saw, he broke out a wicked grin. "Lucky for you, adventure just walked through your door."

"I'm doing just fine on my own, thankyouverymuch," Avery said, embarrassed by the childish huff that ended her words.

Luke's glance across the counter at Cindy was answered with a sad shake of the woman's head. As Avery flushed from head to toe, she vowed to murder her receptionist—as soon as she got Luke out the door.

Those amber eyes swung back to study her. "You sure about that?" he asked.

The intensity of his gaze caught her, held her. His expression was still amused, but gone from his eyes was the teasing, smiling Luke. In the amber depths she saw darkness simmering beneath the surface.

"I keep telling you," Cindy said, "what you need is a nice man who will give you lots of fun without having to resort to stunts like this." She waved the recovered brochure in the air.

With a single lift of his brow, Luke added, "What are the men in this town thinking?"

"They sure don't know what they're missing," Cindy teased.

Had Avery's blush reached lobster levels yet? "I don't need sex to have fun." Oh dear, had she really just said that out loud?

"Nobody said you did, sugar," Luke said. His teeth bit into his full lower lip, but that didn't stop his grin. "But why don't you tell me exactly what kind of adventure you're looking for? I might be able to help."

The ring of the door chime saved her from answering. "Gotta go," she mumbled as she moved, only to stumble over her own feet.

Luke was quick to catch her arm, helping her upright again. "Why don't we talk about it over dinner?" he asked, too soft for anyone else to hear.

Or maybe not. Cindy's happy dance in the background had Avery's face burning once more.

"Nope," she said. "I'm good."

Again his husky voice played along her nerves. "I'm sure you are, but with me it would be better."

Oh, Lordy. Avery almost choked. She wanted nothing more than to get out of here. Forget whoever had come through the door.

Twisting out of Luke's grasp, she chose the other direction and the safety of the therapy room. She threw an "I'm sure you have better things to do," over her shoulder as she escaped, praying she didn't damage her dignity by falling flat on her face.

Heaven help her, Luke Blackstone was gonna be a handful.

* * *

"Has she made you cry like a girl yet?"

Luke quelled his sudden urge to smack his twin. After all, they weren't twelve anymore. "No. There's been no crying." Though his control had been shaky sometimes, he'd held it together. Jacob was teasing, but thankfully he didn't know how close to home his statement hit.

As the oldest brother, Aiden obviously thought he had a say, too. "I thought for sure she'd pulverize you after what you said at the country club."

Of course, someone had to bring that up. "I'm too cute for her not to forgive me."

Aiden smirked, then made a quick retreat behind his desk before Luke's swing could connect. So his restraint hadn't lasted long. He'd always been a big kid.

Unlike Aiden, who looked perfectly at home behind the heavy desk in the study at Blackstone Manor—though the studious furniture and shelves full of books were slightly deceiving. Aiden had been born too big for his britches. Luke's earliest memories were of Aiden being punished in this very room by their grandfather for some teenage rebellion or another. The adult Aiden refused to back down, either. It was there in the artistic tumble of his dark hair and lack of a tie.

His brothers shared a grin that awoke suspicions in Luke's mind. "Spill it."

"Just be careful, that's all," Aiden said.

Luke looked from one to the other, settling on the familiar face of his twin. "What's he mean? What could little ol' Avery do to me?"

"Oh, it's not Avery you need to watch out for," Jacob said. "It's the town."

Huh?

Jacob went on. "Avery is notorious in Black Hills. This entire town has tried to marry her off ever since her mother died. They're relentless."

"Why?"

Aiden smirked. "You've been away from a small town for too long if you have to ask. She's young, pretty and single. Every matron in the county sees her as a princess in need of someone to take care of her."

They both eyed Luke, who quickly held up his hands in surrender. "The last thing I need is a princess." He moved over to one of the long windows, hiding his reaction from the others, because deep inside he couldn't deny his attraction. He could ignore it as long as he wanted, but it was there all the same.

"Just be careful," Jacob said. "They'll marry you off before a first date."

"Not. Me."

His twin just laughed, making him look more like Luke despite his close-cropped hair. "Yeah, right. The princess and the local celebrity—they'd eat that up."

Definitely time to change the subject. "Didn't we meet here to talk about something more important than local gossip? Like this spying job you have for me?"

Aiden choked, so Jacob answered, "Well, I wouldn't call it that."

"Why not? Don't think I can pull off the James Bond bit?" He mimed straightening a suit jacket and tie, just for kicks.

"I don't think he went in for corporate sabotage. A little too tame for him."

Luke shrugged. "Hey, I've got to start somewhere."

Jacob threw up his hands and dropped into one of the chairs, obviously knowing when he'd been verbally outmaneuvered. But Aiden didn't give up. "I'm hoping, if you come in with the stated purpose of inspecting the mill to bring you up to snuff as a full partner, then maybe you'll see something Jacob and I have missed."

The brothers, along with their new head of security, Zachary Gatlin, had been secretly investigating a saboteur who seemed intent on ruining Blackstone Mills. The brothers had eliminated several suspects, but still had no clue who the actual culprit was. Or if they were even still out there. Whoever it was intent on destroying Black Mills would end up destroying the whole town in the process, since they were the biggest supplier of both jobs and housing in the area—heck, the whole county. Without the mill, Black Hills would cease to exist.

It had been a grueling year for his brothers, dealing with all of that on top of Luke's car accident. "Anything new?" Luke asked.

"Nothing I can prove, yet," Jacob said, his amber eyes darkening.

"That sounds promising."

His twin nodded. "Zach has one of his men following the trail, but it looks like we also have some embezzling going on."

"That's bold," Luke said. "The orders, company equipment, our cotton supply and the Manor itself…

now money. Is there anything this guy isn't afraid to put his hands on?"

"Not that we can tell," Aiden said with a slow shake of his head. He pressed his palms against the desktop. "As soon as we cut off one avenue, he finds another. All too easily."

Luke paced across the room despite some lingering muscle pain from his therapy session. His rising anxiety made the walls close in, leaving him eager to move, to escape. An all-too-familiar feeling. "That's disheartening."

"Well," Aiden said, "I hope I can cheer you up with my news."

"Yeah?" the twins said in chorus.

"The legalities of Grandfather's will are all finished. The mill is now mine," Aiden said.

"Wow. That was quicker than you thought," Luke said. "Congratulations."

"It *was* quicker than I thought," Aiden conceded. "But I'm glad, because now I can move on to plan B."

A short glance at Jake didn't provide any clues as to what that might be. He looked as expectant as Luke felt. Aiden pulled a thick envelope out of his inner jacket pocket.

"I've had my personal lawyer pull up this paperwork," he said. "I'm changing the ownership of the mill to all three of us, instead of just me."

Luke simply stared, not fully comprehending.

Jacob spoke for both of them. "But Aiden, this is *your* inheritance."

"It shouldn't be. It should be *ours*. Not just mine. Not a weapon to turn us against each other, as Grandfather intended." He took a solid breath. "A family investment. We're all putting our lives into the mill, the town. We're sharing the responsibility. We should share the benefits."

"Whoa. Wait a minute."

Jacob's smile faded as he looked over at Luke, but Luke couldn't give in just to make his twin happy.

"I'm not staying here," he reminded them. "The only thing I plan on investing my life in is my racing career—the minute I'm cleared to get behind the wheel. I'm here only because I have to be."

Luke could almost feel Jacob's emotions fall along with his expression. Aiden remained more stoic as he said, "You never know what might happen in the future, Luke."

"Is this why you insisted I come home?" Luke asked, panic rising in his chest. "Did you think you could force me home, force me to find something of value here, and then I'd never want to leave? Like you two have?"

He didn't even realize his voice had risen until he stopped talking. The three of them stared at each other in silence. Embarrassment swept over Luke like a heated blanket. Where had that come from? "Look, I'm sorry. I know y'all would never do that to me."

"No, I wouldn't," Aiden agreed quietly. "I would never trick you into coming here. After all, I know very well how that feels."

Their grandfather had faked his own death, bringing Aiden home to care for their sick mother, but it was only a trick to force Aiden and Christina into marrying. Even though the man really was dead now, Aiden faced what James Blackstone had done to him every day. Luckily, he'd been given a happy ending.

Luke didn't want one. Not here.

Aiden wasn't finished. "I'd never force you to sign this paperwork," he said, giving the envelope a little shake. "But that doesn't mean I don't wish you would. Regardless of what your immediate future holds, you're still a part of this family. I hope one day you can willingly put your name on the mill, and reap the benefits along with the rest of your family."

All the work would be done by Aiden and Jacob. They should have the rewards—they *would* have the rewards. And Luke would have his freedom. He loved his brothers, loved the new family they'd built. But how could he stay here and still feed his love for the road?

Unbidden, an image of Avery's face as she flushed with embarrassment came to him. He shook the enticing image away. He had never let anything in Black Hills hold him back. He certainly wasn't going to start now.

He and Avery would have a little fun, something to liven up his time here, but he could still walk away on his own terms. When he was good and ready.

Three

All work and no play made Avery a dull girl and apparently made Luke a frisky boy. Just the look on his face as he settled into one of the treatment rooms warned her he would be trouble.

Avery experienced a lot of feelings during her therapy sessions with clients: pride, sympathy, joy…but never this mixture of irritation and interest. How did he get under her skin with such little effort? A few words and she was tripping over her own feet.

His very presence seemed to inject her with pheromones that clouded her mind and drew her thoughts where they shouldn't go in a professional setting. Especially when her work required her to have her hands all over him.

Then there was the return of the awkwardness. She'd stopped dating because of it. Better to avoid it than to wonder if she had a medical condition—one that caused shaking, clumsiness and unintelligent muttering—all with a single look from any eligible, attractive man. The sight of a handsome man shot her adrenaline up, and if he spoke to her, she immediately became all thumbs. Her considerable intelligence didn't help at all. And her fellow citizens' determination to marry her off meant she'd had a wealth of humiliating experiences.

Dropping things, stumbling into door frames, bumping into all manner of furniture, and—her favorite—jerking her fork so that food ended up in all kinds of crazy places. One time, she'd actually flicked pasta onto her date's eyebrow. She couldn't remember that incident without cringing. So Mark escorted her to many functions, which gave her a reprieve from the matchmaking mamas.

The only time it didn't happen was when she put on her scrubs and became her professional self—comfortable in her knowledge and authority.

Until Luke. And he knew it, too.

Luke—with his sexy stare and flirty ways—jumpstarted the phenomenon quicker than any guy ever had. Which was why she approached him for this second session with her professional facade firmly in place. And it would stay that way. "I've worked up a comprehensive plan for you," she said, "now that I've had a chance to evaluate you firsthand—"

"Firsthand evaluation?" he asked, bending to catch her gaze. "How did I miss that? Can I have a do-over?" His wiggling brows didn't help her nerves. She gripped his chart hard before it could get loose.

"Behave," she said in her sternest voice.

"Oh, honey, I don't know how," he said with a wicked grin that sent shivers racing over her.

How could he derail her so easily, so completely? She dared not speak for a moment, afraid she'd get out no more than a croak as her throat tried to close. That would be humiliating.

Finally, she cleared the constriction. "Look, in this clinic, I'm the boss. This is my career." She adopted a stern look, despite the amusement on his face. "Here, I'm not your friend, family, or—" She almost said *girlfriend*. Where the heck had that come from? "So stop playing and get busy."

He didn't respond right away, which surprised her. Luke always seemed quick on the draw. But she could feel him watching her. Probably preparing for battle.

Lord, have mercy. His teasing made her want to combust from the inside out. Her cheeks burned in a flash fire she couldn't control. She hadn't felt like this since, well, since Luke had jokingly teased her in high school. Good or bad, she wasn't sure. The mixture of irritation and utter fascination with someone who could dive right into the good parts of life while she was left hugging the walls in fear confused her.

"You know what I mean," she finally said, swallowing her emotions down. "We can be friends elsewhere—"

"We can?"

"—but here, business only." Maybe the less she spoke the better. He seemed intent on twisting her words for his own amusement.

"So out there you're fair game?" he asked with a quirk of his brow. Smart-ass.

"Down to work. Now," she said, holding out the folder, open to the plan she'd worked up for him.

"Can I just say one thing before the friendship blackout starts?" he asked.

Knowing anything she said would just encourage him, she simply watched him without responding.

"Look, I wasn't kidding about dinner," he said, bending a little to look her in the eyes.

Startled, she met his gaze without hesitation, getting a spark of deep connection before turning away. "Don't worry about it," she said, hoping to shoo the subject away like an unwelcome bug.

"Look, you said you wanted to have some fun, an adventure—"

"Actually, Cindy said that."

"And I can help."

She remembered his whispered words from the other day. There was no doubt in her mind that any adventure would be incredible with Luke along for the ride. "What are you talking about?"

"Hey, every day is an adventure for me. And I don't need to climb the side of a mountain for a thrill. I'd go so far as to bet that there are some pretty interesting adventures right here close to home that you haven't even thought about."

"And you plan to show them to me?"

He straightened a little. "Why not?"

She couldn't raise her voice above a whisper. "Why are you doing this?"

"In my book, I owe you. I acted like a jerk… before…but I've always seen you as a friend. Besides, this sounds a whole lot more interesting than what I had planned—jaunts over here for my therapist to torture me, and… Nope, that's about it for the next few months." His smile was hopeful. "Let me do this for you."

"I don't know…"

"Scared?"

Heck, yes. "Maybe."

His teasing smirk said he knew he would win. "That's okay. It's all part of the fun."

Suddenly it was all too much—the teasing, the attraction, the nerves. She desperately needed to shift gears. Holding up her hands, she said, "Look, today, we're talking about you. Not me."

"Um, not so far."

"Stop playing and pay attention." Her schoolmarm demands only made him smile wider, but this time he actually cooperated. Miracle of miracles.

That grin said he wasn't finished with her yet, sparking anticipation low in her core, but he finally reached his hand out for the chart.

With relief, she let him read because she didn't have any starch left for her voice.

"This plan is mapped out for ten months."

His unexpected dark tone warned her she might need starch for her backbone, too. "Yes. This is a reasonable prognosis to have you completely healed, strengthened and back on the racing circuit for the season after next."

"That's too long."

She frowned. "But your other therapist projected that from the time of his initial evaluation it could be a year or more before your body is strong enough to return without a risk of further injury. I have to agree."

Luke was shaking his head before she was even half-finished. "Not an option."

She could totally sympathize as the last of the teasing disappeared from his eyes, replaced by frustration. "Our bodies don't always agree to the timelines we want," she reminded him, her voice going soft with sympathy.

"This one damn well better." There was no room for anything but determination in Luke's voice. "I will be back on the racing circuit this next season. No later."

Avery knew when pushing would gain her ground, and this definitely wasn't the time. So she let his remark go. She'd found when men got something in their heads, especially something they were passionate about, there wasn't any argument that would do much good.

And she was frankly relieved that his determination got his focus off her. By the time they moved into the workout room, her control was firmly back in place. A return to the comfortable fit of her therapist persona.

Luke's rippling upper body muscles distracted her at times—clearly he worked out regularly. His body was slim but strong, deceptively so when hidden beneath his clothes. But it met every challenge she gave him and more. His lower body performed, though it was obviously not to his satisfaction.

He gave it his all—she couldn't fault him for not trying. About halfway through the circuit, she started thinking of him as Tough Guy. No matter the demand, he did it without question. He never asked to stop, never cried—almost 90 percent of her patients did in the early days. He just kept pushing forward.

His expression was the most serious she'd seen on him since his return, except for the stoic one she'd glimpsed as he'd made his way across the dining room floor that first night. She'd seen similar expressions on many patients—that determination to ignore the stares, ignore the pain and force yourself to move regardless of your body's protests.

As they came to the end of his session, she bent and twisted his legs, pulling them into positions that would ease the tension, improve his range of motion and hopefully lessen his pain. Time and again she forced her gaze away from glistening muscles and sexy hollows. Not to mention the scars that had her heart cramping in sympathy.

But he'd worked hard today and there was a much better way to help him recover than a simple muscle stimulation session, even though she knew she shouldn't touch him any more than necessary. But it would help. By morning, Luke would appreciate anything that would make it easier for him to get out of bed.

At least, that's the excuse she gave herself.

"Come on," Avery said, urging Luke to his feet after helping him stretch. He'd always had a love/hate relationship with stretching. He'd rather be running or pumping weights, but one of his former trainers had convinced him how good it was for his body. After that, he'd been able to relax into it.

But somehow stretching with Avery was different. It should feel good, did feel good, but not in the way he'd experienced before. Male hands, male strength—his other physical therapist had a no-nonsense touch that did the job at hand and nothing else.

Avery's hands during their sessions gave him a sense of comfort, as if he could feel her desire for him to heal within each touch. Even through the pain he caught a hint of awareness beneath his skin, an itch for more. And always, that low-level hum distracted him.

"Reward time," she said.

Too bad that couldn't mean what his body hoped it did. Nope. It would be the usual post-therapy ritual that included heat and some electrical muscle stimulation to reduce pain and atrophy. Sad when getting shocked was the highlight of his visit.

He assured his disappointed body that this was a good thing. After all, he had rules of his own. Namely, he was not staying in Black Hills—which meant no entanglements. No relationships. His body would simply have to mourn the loss of more intimate contact.

Her rules challenged and intrigued him. Professionalism was very important to her, especially when dealing with a lot of people who had watched her grow up. Still, he longed to break through her professional facade. One, because she needed some fun more than any person he'd met in forever. Someone to push her buttons, force her to loosen up.

Two, he needed a distraction from the first true attraction he'd felt in a long time. Especially since it was toward a woman he would not be able to get away from in the coming months. But they could be friends, right? Just friends.

"So how come I never saw you when I came home?" He chuckled. "It's almost like you were avoiding me."

He almost bumped into her backside as she halted. The odd look she threw over her shoulder smothered his teasing. Had she really—?

"Why would you avoid me?" he asked.

"Do you want your reward?" she countered in a cool tone.

"Um, yeah."

"Then don't ask irrelevant questions."

She just might have found the key to making him fall in line. But that didn't stop him from being curious. He'd bet his racing car that she had avoided him…and didn't want him to know it.

As she walked away, she said, "I guarantee you won't want to miss this."

Just like that, his mouth watered, hunger rising out of nowhere to overwhelm him. It was totally out of character for him, this physical need to be close to someone. If it had been anyone else, he'd have let the hunger lead him, but he couldn't. Not with Avery. Indulging in something physical with her wouldn't be fair, knowing he would never make his home here.

But now curiosity had joined the mix of anticipation and arousal, so he leaned a little heavier on his cane to gain speed. What could be better than the usual after-workout routine? At least it eased the soreness long enough for him to get home. By tomorrow morning, he'd be stiff again. Even the massive whirlpool tub Aiden had installed in his suite didn't help for long. His body resisted what he wanted.

He'd been told he pushed too hard before, but each

moment without definitive recovery ramped up a panic inside. Getting back on the track was a need that called to him day and night. He couldn't rest for the jitters beneath his skin.

An itch to escape.

It only subsided when he was with Avery. With her, he felt a constant, low-level hum that drew his gaze, his attention—hell, his body—in her direction. An illusion that, if he could just get close enough, all the fears and doubts and nerves would stop. Dangerous territory. Which gave him one more reason to keep his hands to himself.

When Avery opened the door to one of the smaller rooms around the perimeter and Luke glimpsed a thickly padded massage table, he wanted to groan. Have mercy. Now he had an itch for something completely different.

"Take off your shoes. I just want to work some of the tension out of your legs and back," she said.

He wanted to joke, to throw something stupid out there to break the tension building under his skin. But nothing came to him. "Is massage an extra perk?" he tried, his voice sounding strained.

A slight choke had him glancing at her with a tight grin, but she'd turned away.

"Um, no," she finally said, though her voice was muffled. It took him a minute to realize she was off balance, uncertain. Did she not normally do this?

That settled him down, and he was able to tease her again. "So am I simply special?"

Her obvious embarrassment was so cute he wanted to kiss it away. Her flushed cheeks and shaky hands made him warm, awoke a need to hug her and share a grin. Not the reaction he was used to, but definitely safer. Shucking his shoes and socks, Luke approached the table with a breathless anticipation that was exponentially higher than the situation warranted.

To his surprise, she launched a comeback. "It's not actually on the fee schedule, but I do need to put my massage therapy license to use now and then."

With those words, every muscle in his body went taut. For someone who already had mobility issues, it was not the best state of affairs. But how could he relax knowing Avery had even more skills in her arsenal that could slay him in an instant? He lay face-down as best he could and breathed through the pain of getting his legs prone. That took his mind off the ache forming in his groin pretty quick.

"Moving a little more slowly would make changing positions easier," Avery chided.

"Can't hide anything from you, huh?"

Her voiced softened as she drew closer. "Oh, I'm a bit more observant than most."

What did she see in him? He was used to projecting the fun-loving, hard-playing athletic image. This wasn't his finest hour. Could she spot the desperation, the bone-deep need to get back behind the wheel? The fear that lingered beneath his determination? His thoughts opened up a dark cave he'd rather not explore.

The sound of a cabinet door broke the silence, then familiar heat blanketed his upper back in a thick weight. His whole body automatically melted into the cloth-covered table beneath him. Then Avery's hands found the small of his back and thinking ceased—he could only feel.

Definitely not like a dude. He'd never before had a therapeutic massage where he had to bite his lip to keep from begging his masseuse for more. Hell, her technique was flawless. Now his body wanted to take this far away from the office to a much more private setting.

Yep, he was in a heap of trouble here.

Those slender fingers traced and kneaded every inch of every muscle on his legs and lower back. Every one except the one he wanted her to touch with an ache that was inherently male. Trapped beneath him, that essential part of his body throbbed in an attempt to gain attention. Luke was grateful for the safeguard, even while he reveled in the return of his body's most basic demands. So much better than his struggle with fear and loathing.

He'd enjoyed a steady stream of sexual encounters until the accident. But why did this feel like the perfect unique blend of innocence and sensuality to spur his body into hyperdrive?

Oh, yeah, she was definitely trying to torture him.

Her fingers traced over muscles, hills, and into valleys. Smoothing out the tension, working out the knots, drawing out the moans. This girl had some hidden talents.

"You have magic fingers," he moaned.

She dug particularly deep into his thigh.

"Ouch, woman."

"Behave." The prim schoolteacher voice was back. Not the direction he was looking for.

"It was a compliment. I swear."

He lifted a little to glance over his shoulder, only to find her cheeks flushed, eyes a little heavy-lidded.

But all of it disappeared when her gaze met his. Then one brow lifted and her lips pressed together.

Even as he settled back in place, the image of that aroused look on her refined features wouldn't disappear from his mind. That expression like she'd enjoyed touching him as much as he'd enjoyed being touched. It was a temptation he didn't need. Then the slide of her hands transformed from a baker kneading dough to the skilled glide of a woman savoring the skin beneath her fingers.

The very air around him grew heavy. His breath sped up to match his heartbeat. Could this torture continue forever? But certain parts of him demanded it end quickly, in a very satisfying way. Time to change the tempo.

"You never did say why I haven't seen you around…"

He left the sentence hanging, hoping to introduce some sane conversation before he went out of his everlovin' mind. She paused midstroke, his thigh muscle twitching before she continued again.

"I didn't really socialize much until my mother died," she said, her voice low. "There wasn't really time—or rather, when there was, I was too exhausted to care. I stuck close to home mostly. And establishing a practice takes a lot of work, even with the ready-made clientele here."

Which was no doubt true, even if he still sensed a cover-up. His heartbeat slowed as he focused on her. "I'm sure she was very grateful for all you did for her."

"I know she was. She told me every day."

Luke thought of his own mother, Lily, who had been comatose since a stroke. She'd already sustained injuries from a car accident that had left her unable to walk. There'd been more than once that Luke had wished his mother could tell them something, anything to let them know she was okay—even if it was goodbye. But she couldn't.

"You're lucky," he mumbled, then realized how callous that might sound and glanced over his shoulder.

Avery met his look, understanding in her gentle eyes. "I know."

She pressed her palms flat against his skin, sending that tingle through him once more. A confusing mix of arousal and comfort.

Some people didn't know, could never understand what it was like to lose a parent…but not really lose them. To wish so badly that you could speak to them, but realize it would never happen again. But Avery understood. Her observant ways had probably told her far more about the situation than anyone else knew.

Then she threw him into the fire. "What about you? Did you ever think you'd be moving back here, even for a temporary hiatus?"

Luke was glad his face didn't show. Being home was still a touchy subject for him—more than he wanted anyone to know. "Nope."

"But it's better now, right?"

His body stilled even more. "How did you know?"

"Everyone knows James Blackstone was a difficult man—"

"Try demon…"

"—but the way he treated you boys was unconscionable."

He shouldn't ask. He really shouldn't. "How did you know?"

"Just from the sheer amount of time I spent watching those around me. It's amazing what people will say in front of you when they don't realize you're there."

Ouch. Despite the magic of her fingers, Luke rolled to his side. "Did we really do that to you, Avery? Ignore you? Make you feel invisible?"

"Luke, y'all weren't the only ones. I was shy, and worked very hard to fade into the woodwork. Do it often enough, and people expect it."

He remembered seeing her walk across the country club dining room and realized just how far she'd come. That walk was probably as hard for her as his own had been. "How did you become so smart?"

"Smart? No. Just…practical."

"Practical, huh? Doesn't that ever get boring?"

This conversation was way deeper than he'd planned.

She shook her head, a slight smile tilting the corners of her pink bow lips. "No," she said. "There isn't time to be bored."

He wanted to ask if she felt the same way in the dark of night, when she was home alone with no one to laugh and cuddle with, but he didn't. He couldn't.

The deep stuff wasn't what he was here for.

"Let's get you set up for your next appointment," she said as she moved away from the table.

The fun was over.

Flipping over on the narrow table proved harder than he thought, but at least he had the coward's comfort of knowing Avery faced away from him. Easier was getting himself upright with his legs hanging off the table. Boy, her magic hands had turned his muscles to jelly.

When Avery turned back, she was studying his chart. He could have called her on avoiding him, but he let it go. For now.

She was back to being all business. "Let's shoot for three days a week."

"Sure." Not like he had much else going on. "However often it takes."

"That means we will see each other on Friday. Monday, Wednesday, Friday good for you?"

He nodded. Deep in his brain, he searched for a way to instigate himself into other parts of her life. She might have forgotten about him helping her have fun, but he hadn't. "We could see each other before then. You know, for dinner?"

"Are we back to that again?" she asked, her face completely blanking for a moment.

"Mary makes a mean prime rib up at Blackstone Manor. Why don't you join me? I could even ask her to make her famous chocolate chip cookies."

Avery frowned, shifting the chart in her hands. "I don't think that's a good idea."

"Why not?" Luke had a pretty decent puppy-dog look when he tried.

"It's just, um…"

Yep, the look was working.

She swallowed. "With me being, you know, your physical therapist, maybe socializing isn't such a good idea."

"Why not? Because you said everything outside of the office was fair game."

Her face flushed and he knew he'd gotten her. "That's not what I meant and you know it."

His male instincts urged him to stalk closer, crowd her in and make her admit she was just as attracted to him as he was to her. Instead he forced himself to remain still, using words to reel her in. "Come on. You want an adventure. I want to help you find one. Let's talk about it over dinner."

"Well…" Her flush deepened, but she also straightened her shoulders. "I guess I could do dinner one night."

Was that a slight squeak he heard in her voice? "Good. I know Christina has been dying to see you, too."

A little of the starch drained from her posture. "Oh, um, yes. That sounds nice."

Obviously she hadn't been to a dinner with all of them home. *Nice* wasn't the word he'd use. *Chaotic*, maybe. Just what she needed.

"It will be interesting, to say the least." Not like the gloom and doom his grandfather had presided over. James Blackstone had demanded the appearance of a family dinner, but they had been mostly silent events with none of the laughing, joking and talking Luke associated with that idea. Especially not since his mother's car accident.

As he came to his feet, the quizzical little smile Avery gave distracted him. He saw nothing else. Not taupe walls, nor yellow scrubs. Just pale blue eyes and bow-shaped lips moving closer as she stepped forward.

Before he could reach for his cane, his legs gave him the old heave-ho and collapsed. Avery had moved

close, too close to miss out on his game of Timber.
Down they both went.

He tried to twist, but his body wouldn't cooperate.
They hit the floor hard. Or rather, Avery did. Luke's
arms worked better than his legs, catching him before
he landed on her. *Oh, that elbow was gonna bruise.*
Of course, the rest of his body couldn't help but tangle all up in hers.

They came to rest hip to hip, stomach to stomach,
and all of Luke's pent-up need was blatantly evident.
Once more, the first thing that popped into his head
came out of his mouth, even though he knew he'd
pay for it later.

"Sweetheart, you're the softest landing place I've
had in a while." The scary part—it was true.

Four

For once, Luke was able to walk into breakfast at Blackstone Manor like a normal person, albeit relying on his cane, instead of a hunched-over hobbit moaning in pain. He tossed Christina a grin as he approached the breakfast dishes on the mahogany sideboard.

Though she seemed a little pale and not her usual serene self this morning, she returned his smile. "Someone's looking much better than the last time I saw him," she teased.

Since neither of his brothers were there to rag him, Luke spoke freely. "I swear that woman has magic in her fingers."

"I bet."

Without thought, Luke whipped his head around, pinning her with a glare until he realized she was joking with him. *Busted*.

Christina raised her hands in surrender. "Just kidding." But that smug smile said she'd gotten all the information she needed.

The pressure to explain rose. For once, he gave in. Maybe if he talked some of his thoughts out, he could make more sense of them. Somehow, he could share with Christina things he'd normally keep to himself. He attributed it to her peaceful bedside manner. His brother Aiden was one of the few people who could shake her calm attitude.

Yet he was grateful to be filling his plate as he spoke, instead of facing her across the lace-covered table. "Avery gave me a massage after my session yesterday. My muscles haven't felt this good since *before* my accident."

"Nice," she murmured. Again she tossed him the knowing look, but thankfully she held her teasing. "She worked on my shoulder once. Definitely skilled. I'm glad she could help you out."

Why did he remember his *therapeutic* massage with less-than-clinical nuances? He shouldn't…he knew he shouldn't. Trying to shake the memory, he finished filling his plate and settled across the table from Christina.

She went on. "This is the most pain-free I've seen you since you moved back."

Luke was a little shocked himself.

Christina studied her plate for a moment. "I know it seems silly to be worried about a grown woman, but Avery has pulled away some since KC and I became involved with your brothers. Maybe hanging out with us makes her feel like a third wheel. But I think Avery needs someone to shake her out of her rut, so to speak." She gave Luke one of her patented purposeful looks.

He didn't disappoint. "Well, I do need a hostess for dinner."

Christina lowered her fork despite the bite of waffle on the end. "She agreed?"

"Yes. She tried to brush me off, so I told her how much you missed her...and how disappointed you would be if she didn't come."

He leaned back in his chair, accompanied by a creak of wood. Part of him wanted to confess how conflicted he was, how much he wanted Avery to come to dinner for himself. He didn't want to admit to the attraction that grew every time he saw her, but he was drawn to the chance to make the laughter, the spark of life in Avery's eyes grow.

"She's funny—so dedicated to her work, holding fast to this therapist-patient bit. But I think she needs someone to push her outside her safety zone." A cohort in crime, so to speak. Luke didn't want Christina to know how desperate he was for the job.

The whole time he spoke, Christina's expression grew in excitement until she practically glowed. "So you are interested! I knew it."

Uh-oh. Christina would be unbearable once she thought she was right.

"No, ma'am." He would not let anything sexual even start between him and Avery. Not when he had no plans to hang around. She was obviously rooted in this town, and the last thing he could see himself as was a small town husband. "You can put that emerging matchmaker back in her cage, because it's not gonna happen." He waved his arms around the room. "This version of happily-ever-after is not for me."

"That's what Aiden and Jacob said," she mumbled beneath a smile.

"I'm serious, Christina." Christina's astute look had him adding, "I just want to be her friend. I owe her that." And much, much more. Even though he'd brushed her off as a teenager for all the right reasons, he still felt bad about it now.

"As long as you're careful with her," Christina gave the obligatory warning, but Luke could see her concern for her friend in her darkened eyes. "Honestly, she deserves more than a little bit of fun after all she's been through."

"Has it been rough since her mother died?"

"Oh, it was rough way before that." Christina shifted the pieces of waffle on her plate as a thoughtful look softened her face.

"How come I haven't heard anything about her when I've been home?"

"Because there wasn't much to hear. She went to college and things were good until the summer after her sophomore year. Then her mother was diagnosed with cancer. She'd been dating a guy pretty steadily, but when she buckled down to finish her studies early, he lost interest."

Ouch. Just what she needed—someone who abandoned her the minute she needed support.

Christina stared into space as she spoke. "She was home as much as her studies would allow, but she finished within a year and a half. Came home and started to build her clientele while taking care of her mom full-time."

"How long was her mom sick?"

"She went into remission once, for a couple of years, I think?" Christina shook her head, sending her thick, dark hair swinging. "She died almost two years ago."

Wow. "That's a long time to be a caregiver."

"Yeah," Christina whispered, trailing off into silence that was punctuated by the clink of their silverware. Finally she said, "She's given her all for Black Hills, but she deserves more—just for herself. I'm glad to see she isn't going to settle."

Luke thought of dinner and Avery's lack of response to Mark's hand at her back. "You mean that Mark guy?"

"Don't get me started," Christina groaned.

"Please don't," Aiden added as he strolled into the room. "Her opinion is less than stellar, I assure you."

A pang stung Luke's chest as Aiden kissed Christina on the temple, but he shook his head. Absolutely no touchy-feely stuff for him. No, sir. Settling down was not in his current timeline.

"Avery and Mark have gone to a lot of functions together since her mother died. I think it started out as convenient, especially for her, since she gets comments about a single woman needing to get married all the time, but I think he's always been more interested than she realizes."

Luke tried to ignore the burn of something unpleasant building in his gut. He hadn't known they'd actually been such a "thing." Part of him did not like that thought...*at all*.

"I've never cared for him, but Aiden says there aren't any complaints at work," Christina went on.

"There aren't," Aiden agreed. He shook his head. "He's perfectly adequate at his job. Of course, adequate and not exemplary is what has kept him where he is at the moment. I can't judge the guy based on feminine intuition."

When Christina threw him a sideways glance, Aiden grinned. "Even if it's coming from one of the smartest, sexiest women I know."

She rolled her eyes as her husband kissed her cheek. "I'll accept the compliment," she said, "but I just haven't ever been able to get past it." With a glance at Luke, she said, "When Mark started pressuring for more—that's when she broke it off."

"How long ago?" Luke asked, keeping his gaze trained on Aiden while he fixed his plate so Christina wouldn't see how much the thought bothered him.

"About six weeks ago, maybe?"

Had that pressure for more than she wanted to deliver been a wake-up call, urging her to break out of her inertia?

Aiden added his two cents worth as he took his seat. "Avery is a very hard worker. When she isn't treating patients, she's helping with fund-raisers or volunteering with local charities. All kinds of community stuff."

Was that because she truly wanted to be busy…or because she just didn't want to go home alone?

"I think—" Christina began.

"—and you would know," Aiden teased, smoothing a hand over his wife's hair.

Christina raised an eyebrow in what Luke liked to call her "lady of the manor" look. "Of course I would. She's one of my best friends and a great person. She deserves some happiness after all she's lost. Someone to help her loosen up and have fun—like KC did for Jacob."

Aiden shook his head. "She may have loosened him up too much. Do you know he actually took a day off work last week? Just because?"

Luke grinned as Christina smacked Aiden's arm. A day off for a workaholic like Jacob was a freakin' miracle.

"I think I can handle that." Not the romantic part, he reminded himself. Luke felt compelled to specify so Christina wouldn't get any ideas about forever. "While I'm home, it'll be my mission to teach her all about good ol' fun."

Aiden winked at Christina. "Sounds like a worth-while mission to have."

She nodded. "Since her mother died, her only fun has been charity events, community stuff. She needs something for *her*."

"Can. Do," Luke said. "Starting with dinner."

Christina simply stared. "I thought for sure you'd be more adventurous than that."

"You know me so well. But trust me, this is just the beginning." That rock climbing brochure might be what Avery *thought* she wanted…but Luke knew exactly what he was doing. He swallowed down a big bite of homemade waffles, licking syrup off his top lip. "Do we still have that old tire swing around here somewhere?"

Five

Why did going to dinner at a friend's house spark uncomfortable butterflies in her stomach? Avery had been to Blackstone Manor many times before, but this felt different.

Yes, Luke would be here. Yes, he had invited her. But it was a family dinner, for goodness' sake.

In all the years she'd been coming to Blackstone Manor to see Christina—and even before that for social events as a teenager—Avery had always been greeted at the door by the Blackstone butler, Nolen. Tonight the heavy door with its lion knocker swung back to reveal Luke.

As a concession to the cooling night air, he wore khakis with a smooth, deep blue polo shirt that made his amber eyes almost glow in contrast. His blond hair, longer than his twin's, was stylishly disheveled.

He'd probably just dried it with a towel, applied a quick comb and been done. His casual good looks took her breath away.

Avery always felt like she was trying too hard. She'd give anything for a set of yellow scrubs right now, instead of her casual black jeans and thin gray sweater with a bright blue argyle pattern down the center. At least then she'd feel more in control than she did right now, with him eyeing her from head to toe. Professional distance might be the only thing to save her sanity in the face of this undeniable draw to Luke Blackstone.

Heaven help her.

As jitters set in, she eyed the door frame while she approached in an effort not to catch it with her shoulder. *Careful.* Luke's grin widened just a touch, as if he knew exactly what she was thinking.

Then—*oompf.*

Avery stumbled over the doorstep, tripping as momentum propelled her forward until she landed right in Luke's outstretched arms. He mumbled something. She wasn't sure what, because her senses narrowed down to the warm, spicy scent of his skin and the heat of his hands as they rested against her back. He pressed her closer, making her feel at once safe and unbridled.

Then reality returned. She jerked upright, only to be held in place by his embrace. A sneaking glance found his amber eyes filled with laughter.

"Are you trying to throw yourself at me?" he asked.

As if she could coordinate her limbs to do that on purpose.

She searched for her strictest voice. "I was simply testing your stability. That's all." *Oh, could this floor open up and swallow me?* Her heart raced as his hands inched back until they rested on her upper arms.

He wasn't quite convinced. "Uh-huh." Then he fingered a strand of her hair. "Gorgeous."

Startled, she remembered this was one of the few occasions she'd worn it completely down. A ponytail was a necessity for work, especially with the thickness of her hair. For most formal occasions she wore an elegant, upswept hairdo because it kept the thick mass out of her face and she could accessorize it with jeweled combs and such. But tonight, facing the mirror and seeing the same old, same old, she'd opted to leave it loose around her face.

Suddenly a masculine voice filled the foyer. "Master Luke, is that the proper way to answer the door?" Nolen asked. His voice remained completely deadpan, but Avery could swear his knowing eyes twinkled.

She stepped back, only to hear Luke's cane clatter as it fell to the floor. "Oh, no," Luke said as she bent to sweep it up. "That was most improper of me. I should be fired, Nolen. On the spot."

Turning toward the butler, Avery smiled. "Completely my fault, Nolen. I'm so clumsy sometimes." Even now her knees shook. She couldn't tell if it was from her almost-fall, or from being close enough to sniff Luke Blackstone. His clean, warm scent lingered on her clothes, though it seemed as though she hadn't been close nearly long enough for that to be possible.

"A gentleman never lays the blame with a woman," Nolen said. "Welcome, Miss Avery."

"Thank you, Nolen."

"Yes," Luke murmured. "Welcome."

How could just the tone of his voice make her every cell sit up and beg for attention? The simple words were spoken low and smooth. But his sexy, teasing tone lingered over her, becoming absorbed within the earlier sensations and fogging her brain for a moment.

With a quick shake of her head, she carefully stepped forward, following Nolen through the breeze-way into the front parlor. Another fall would be too embarrassing for words. She could feel the emotions burning on her fair cheeks. Hopefully it wasn't too noticeable as she hugged Christina in greeting.

Tonight should have been like any other night that she'd joined the Blackstones for dinner. Casual conversation among friends. Mary's wonderful food and fine wine. But as they chatted, then moved into the elegant dining room and were served, a constant awareness hummed beneath Avery's skin.

It didn't help that Luke seemed to have developed a fascination with her hair. She caught him studying it more than once, with a sort of longing on his face that made her breath catch. Even when Luke wasn't paying her direct attention, the feeling remained. What would he do if she actually responded to his teasing with interest? Would he run for the hills? Laugh?

Kiss her?

She shouldn't think like that. It would never happen. Not for a girl like her. He simply liked to joke and play games. She was something to alleviate his boredom. That's all. Instead she tried to focus on the conversation flowing around her.

The Blackstone brothers began talking about the horrible incidences of sabotage that had threatened to put Blackstone Mills out of business over the last year. Avery had closely watched the drama unfold, along with the rest of the community.

She couldn't help asking, "Do you think it's over? Or is someone just waiting out there for another opportunity?" That thought sent shivers over her, though she was far from the target. How could someone in their community work so hard to tear the very people who supported it apart?

"Let's just say I'm cautiously optimistic," Aiden said, though he wore a slight frown that fit his dark good looks. "We've been without a major incident for two months now. Since the cotton crop debacle."

Avery remembered the widespread gossip and panic when Zachary Gatlin, now the Blackstones' head of security, had flown the plane that sprayed the majority of the county's cotton crop with defoliant long before it was ready. He'd maintained his innocence, stating he'd been framed by someone who had secretly switched out the chemicals in the tanks, but small towns bred distrust.

Jacob shook his head. "This lull makes me suspicious. Worried. I have a feeling whoever did this isn't done yet."

Though he and Jacob looked a lot alike, apparently Luke had his own opinion that fell somewhere in the middle. "Maybe he figured out we're gonna fix whatever he breaks, instead of abandoning the mill or the town. Might as well hit the road, Jack."

The other two didn't look convinced. Neither did

Christina, but she said, "Worrying about it won't help. We have to keep living, keep working, while continuing to implement the tightest security we can for now. If we let our guard down, one of our employees could pay the price."

Or one of us. The words were unspoken, but even Avery could feel their impression. Whoever the saboteur had been, he'd struck out at each of the Blackstone brothers in turn. Almost fatally in Aiden's case, when an attempt to burn down his sculpting studio occurred with Christina trapped inside. Avery looked at Luke, and prayed he wouldn't become another target in whatever game this crazy person was playing.

"Thank goodness Zach agreed to put his military training to good use," Jacob said.

"Amen," KC said. "Now, can we talk about something more pleasant, please?" Jacob's fiancée handed their son, Carter, over to his dad so she could dig into her lasagna without baby fingers in her plate.

"What do you suggest, my dear?" he asked in a sotto voice that earned him a raised eyebrow.

But Christina quickly filled the gap. "How about the Christmas dinner and dance?" she said, a pleading look coming over her elegant features. "Avery, you must help. Taking this event from the country club to the civic ballroom and opening it up to the public has increased interest by leaps and bounds. Which is great for fund-raising, but not so great on its organizers..." Her voice trailed off as she and KC shared a look.

KC nodded, a crease appearing between her eyebrows. "Especially since one of those organizers has never done anything fancy before. I'm much more comfortable with county fairs and hoedowns."

"It'll be fun," Christina reassured her friend. "I promise."

And it would be. Avery always had a good time coordinating the fund-raisers that helped sustain and build their community. A new playground. School support. A new building for the senior center. They were fun and helped her feel like she was contributing something worthwhile, like her life meant something more than her just working day in and day out. But she couldn't help wondering if—when—there would be something more.

"I'm trying to talk Lucas into helping me with a little side project," Christina said.

Oh, this sounded interesting. Luke's glare across the table told Avery how he felt about it.

"No," he said. "I'd be horrible."

Christina had her protests all lined up. "Why? You're great in front of a camera, with your hundred-watt charm. You've got experience from being interviewed many, many times. Heck, this would even be scripted—sort of."

"Sort of?" Luke's brow shot sky high. "You want me to appear on camera with a dozen or so little kids. How the heck is that gonna be scripted?"

The other brothers laughed. Avery suppressed a grin of her own. Luke always appeared one hundred percent comfortable in front of a camera…but with a bunch of kids? That seemed like a recipe for disaster. She didn't know a single child that was predictable.

Christina leaned forward against the edge of the

table. "It's to help with the fund-raising efforts for the new pediatric ER. Imagine how much exposure we could get statewide with you on the screen."

"I realize I'm a handsome devil," Luke conceded with a smirk that quickly disappeared. "But, no."

Avery happily stepped into the fray. Having something to tease Luke about was fun, since it was usually the other way around. "Come on, Mr. Big Shot. Surely you aren't afraid of a few grimy fingers and wet diapers?"

The incredulous look he shot her sent her into giggles. She had this mental image of Luke standing tall while dozens of kids swarmed him from all sides, climbing him like he was a mountain. Talk about an adventure.

"I'm not good with kids," he insisted. "I barely know what to do with this one."

He gestured to little Carter, sitting proud in his daddy's lap. As if realizing all eyes were on him, the little boy gurgled. The sound and his golden curls were sweetness overload.

"Well, you better figure it out quick," Aiden said. "We'll have another here soon for you to practice on."

For just a moment, the light reflecting off the hundreds of crystal teardrops on the chandelier was too hot, too bright for Avery. Then the room erupted into smiles and congratulations as Christina glowed with happiness. Avery thought that was the biggest grin she'd ever seen on Aiden's face. The normally stoic businessman only softened around his wife, but he'd soon have another reason to let down that infamous guard.

As Avery watched the family rejoice, she couldn't help but compare their happiness to her own barren life. She had friends aplenty, but no one to go home to. No life events on the horizon. She looked at Luke, so full of vitality despite his accident and all the hard work he had to do just to return to normal– – and wanted a taste of that experience.

Surely she deserved a little taste.

But she wouldn't get even a nibble in Black Hills. After all, Luke wasn't a wedding-and-babies kind of guy. Why should he be? A baby meant roots, staying put, not a lifetime in perpetual motion. It was a reminder Avery needed, but it still made her sad. Why? She couldn't say, but the feeling lingered.

"Luke, you'll be a great uncle…again," Christina said.

He would. Luke could charm the warts off a toad. Even when it was a tantrum-throwing toddler. Even if he didn't know it yet.

Just like he charmed her, no matter how many times she hid behind her professionalism. She'd wondered earlier if he would run screaming if she responded in kind, teased and flirted instead of trying to steer him back on a straighter road.

Maybe it was time to shuck the scrubs and embrace an overload of adventure.

Luke could almost feel the moment Avery decided it was time to leave.

KC and Jacob had excused themselves earlier to put Carter to bed. They didn't always stay at Blackstone Manor, preferring the privacy of KC's little house closer to town, but tonight they were using their suite on the third floor.

Conversation between the remaining four of them slowed. No more exciting baby news or community improvement plans, thank goodness. Seated so close to her on a couch in the front parlor, Luke felt tension creep over Avery. Her shoulders pulled up slightly and her hands rubbed against her jeans along the front of her thighs. Even though his brain said to let the evening come to its natural end, the rest of him didn't want her to walk out the door.

He stood, leaning nonchalantly on his cane as he faced her. "Walk with me."

"Oh, I should probably get going." Avery avoided his gaze, but also didn't look at Christina or Aiden. Obviously she hadn't registered that his statement wasn't a question.

Since he wasn't the type to go all caveman, he forced himself to play the hated invalid card... "I kinda figured my physical therapist would encourage me to walk, keep from stiffening up and all—"

Her delightfully creamy skin flushed from collar to cheekbones. "Oh, right."

Those funny nerves that hit her from time to time made an appearance, leaving Luke afraid she might trip again. But he could see the professional mask cover her expression as she consciously slipped behind it. She could think she was in control all she wanted—until he was ready for her to know otherwise. Would he ever get her to relax with him? For him alone?

The women did that huggy thing, then Luke preceded Avery across the breezeway back to the dining room. He led her through the swinging door to the adjacent kitchen. Mary and Nolen were cleaning up the last of dinner.

"Mary," Avery said, "dinner was absolutely delicious. And whatever that chocolate dessert was—yum!"

The older woman grinned. "Well, I had something a little simpler planned, but such big news warranted an extraspecial dessert, you know."

Luke should have known Mary would have the 411 before everyone else in the house. He wasn't sure how, but Mary and Nolen knew everything that went on in Blackstone Manor—no matter how secret it might be.

Mary wiped her hands and hurried over for a hug. "So you have to tell me—how are you, girl?"

"I'm good," Avery said with a smile.

Behind the older woman with her Kiss the Cook apron, Luke spied an entire rack of little beauties cooling down. Mary's infamous chocolate chip cookies. He drew in a deep breath. Yep, chocolate was definitely in order tonight.

"Does my favorite cook have anything left for me?" he asked.

The woman eyed him with the same suspicion she had when he was a teenager up to no good. "There's only one thing worth you nosing around my kitchen," she said. "If I let you have one chocolate chip cookie, then all the other men want one, and on it goes."

"But they've already had dessert," he argued. "It should be safe."

He wasn't pulling anything over on Mary. "So have you, Lucas Blackstone. But I guess I can make an exception for ya."

She scooped a couple of cookies off the cooling rack and set them on napkins before handing them each one. Nolen frowned. "What about me?"

Mary's brow shot up. "When you finish your work, you can have one, too."

The butler muttered as he headed back through the door to the dining room, leaving them all smiling. Mary turned back to Avery. "So everything going okay? The clinic is doing well?"

Luke saw Avery blossom beneath the older woman's attention. "It sure is. How're those hips doing?"

"Good, thanks to you." Mary glanced over at Luke with the wisdom of ages in her eyes. "This girl works wonders, you know."

He remembered that heavenly massage. "Oh, I'm getting the picture."

Mary pointed in his direction. "You see you do everything she says, and it'll all work out fine."

"Yes, ma'am."

The words were forced as Luke's mind flooded with Avery's warnings to wait another season to return to racing. He wanted to push the concern away, but it kept resurfacing—especially at night when he lay in bed, legs aching from the day's exertions.

Luke knew his body. He could return to tip-top shape by February. He had to believe that. The question was, could he prove it to everyone else? Only he understood the danger of losing his worth the longer he was away from the track. Why wait and have to rebuild his reputation when he could come back sooner and stay on top?

All of his hard work up to this point *would not* be for nothing.

Luke's thoughts distracted him as they finished their cookies, then stepped out the back door into the cooling fall air. Avery snuggled into her light leather jacket as the slight breeze ruffled the long strands of her hair. The varying shades of blond, the highlights visible even in the dark, fascinated him. All Luke's memories of her were with her hair up or back. He'd known her ponytail was thick, but never realized just how full and glossy her hair would be in its unfettered glory.

Down as it was now, it transformed into a waterfall of pure temptation. Luke's palms itched to dig in, experience that silkiness against his skin. A groan slipped out unbidden, whisked away by the night air.

"Are you okay?" Avery asked. "Should we go back inside?"

"No, I'm fine." If no one counted the throbbing ache behind his zipper.

"Do you like being back?" she asked, her voice quiet.

"It's okay," he said, leading her down the gentle slope of the lush back lawn, past heirloom iris beds that were only greenery now. "Every nomad needs a home base, right?"

"Doesn't North Carolina feel like home to you?"

Nothing really did. "I have an apartment there, but I wouldn't really call it home. A place to stay, maybe."

She gestured back toward Blackstone Manor, impressively handsome despite the dim light. "Here, neither? Even with your brothers both home?"

"No. I mean, Aiden and Jacob gutted Grandfather's suite on the second floor so I'd have a convenient space—but it isn't really mine."

"I'm sorry," she murmured.

"Why?"

After a moment's pause, she said, "I'd be lost without my house, and I hate that you don't have the same comfort." She was quiet for a few steps before she went on. "A lot of people asked why I didn't sell it after Mom died. Move closer to the clinic. After all, it's way too big for a woman all alone." Her laugh was a huff in the air. "An old maid—I'm sure they say when I'm not around."

"Honey, you're as far from a typical old maid as a woman can get." He reached out to touch that hair, rubbing a small swath between his finger and thumb.

He knew she felt him from the slight hesitation of her body and words, but then she continued walking without looking his way.

"That house has been the one constant in my life. I've been through a lot of bad times there, but also my best. I don't want to let it go. Guess that makes me overly sentimental, huh?"

"Not at all." Without thought, Luke said, "If I called anywhere home, it would be my garage. Crazy, I know, but I'd rather be there than anywhere."

"Makes perfect sense to me, Luke," Avery whispered.

She paused, looking up at the night sky. It was chilly, but clear, with stars in abundance. Luke didn't care. He was too busy soaking up Avery's shadowy profile.

When had this conversation turned so serious? He should be concentrating on fun—not home and hearth.

Finding her arm in the dark, he let his hand slip

down to grasp hers. "Come here," he said, changing their direction toward the nearby oak tree. Massive in size, family lore said it had been there since they settled this land many years ago. Now other trees kept it company, including a couple of magnolias and a pretty old weeping willow, but the oak stood above them all.

Luke and Avery slipped below the bottommost branches to the sheltered circle beneath the tree.

"How pretty," she breathed, as a small amount of moonlight dappled through the leaves.

Luke led her around to the other side where Aiden had helped him hang the tire swing. Now the fun would really begin. "Ever play on one of these?"

"Hmm…no, can't say that I have."

Her dubious tone thrilled him. Even in the dark, he could feel her eyeing him as if he needed to be watched. He might be heading for craziness, after all. That was fine. The more she resisted, the sweeter the surprise when she gave in.

"Never?" he challenged. "Come on. When was the last time you sat on a swing? Any swing?"

Her sigh sounded long-suffering, as if she were indulging him. "When I was a kid, I guess."

"Then it's way past time. Hop on."

"What?" She took a few steps back. "Me? No."

"Yes," he said in a singsong voice. "I dare you."

"Luke, I'm not dressed for a tire swing."

Oh, she was reaching for excuses now. "What? They're pants, at least. Besides, getting dirty makes it a lot more fun."

He hadn't meant his words to come out quite like

that, or for desire to deepen his voice, but his fascination with her was outstripping his control.

"Come on, where's that little adventurer that's trying to break free?" he goaded.

That did the trick, because she moved in his direction. Yes, one hesitant step at a time, but she was moving toward the swing instead of away from it. *Baby steps.*

She stood next to the tire for long moments, then Luke heard a small laugh. "You're gonna find this hilarious, I'm sure," she said, "but I don't even know how to get on this thing."

He moved close, resting his free hand against the small of her back. Just that simple touch was as electric as her falling into his arms earlier. He let the forbidden thrill move through him, savoring it for just a moment.

"Well, you can climb on top and ride." He paused, clearing his throat. When had something so simple become so riddled with innuendos? "Or you can slide your legs through the middle."

And sit on that delectable rear of hers. He did not need to think about her anatomy right now or he'd end up in a world of hurt.

Avery, of course, chose the safer option of sitting in the middle. Luke held the tire steady for her, then moved into position behind her back.

"Don't you dare push me," she said, looking over her shoulder. "You'll hurt yourself."

Luke gave a playful growl but a growl nonetheless. "Don't tell me what to do, woman. My body is operational in all the places I need it to be."

Let her think about that for a while. He let his cane

fall to the ground and grasped the tire on either side of her. His balance held steady as he got her moving. Avery caught her breath with the first swoop. Luke grinned. The sound lent strength to his pushes, making her soar.

For long moments, the only thing heard was the creak of the rope, the rustle of leaves in the tree and the sound of their breath. Then something new joined in—slow at first, but gathering speed. The sound of her enjoyment, laughter mixed with a sort of breathlessness that radiated in his soul.

He had a vivid memory of that same sensation, the first time he could remember feeling it. His first time behind the wheel, alone in a car. Following the road to the deserted outskirts of town, and indulging in his need for speed. He hadn't reached racing heights, or even come close, but it had been his first taste, leaving him hungry for more.

With each push her breath caught, then laughter sprung forth as she reached the apex and hung suspended a moment before rushing back down. He backed up to give her more room, just enjoying the show. Her indulgence lit him up inside, mixing with lingering passion. Almost as if he were living vicariously through her.

No. He'd always lived his own life, on his own terms. But he could still enjoy her journey, right?

So he let the sound of her flow over him, through him—letting his eyes slip closed to hold it inside. Then a small cry and *wham*!

The weight against his chest toppled his balance. Luckily he'd been trained to fall. His body instinctively rolled along one side rather than slam down, but he lay disoriented for a moment. Within seconds he heard feet running in his direction.

"Luke? Luke, are you hurt?"

Avery's breathlessness only made him want to take her breath away in a whole other manner. The warmth of palms meeting his pants-clad legs and seeking upward took his own breath away. He peeked at her. "If I say yes, can I get a massage?"

She loomed closer. "Are you kidding me?"

He ignored her exasperated tone, the dull pain in his hips, and focused on the red of her full lips in the darkness and the wealth of hair like a waterfall as she leaned over him. There was no stopping himself. No talking himself out of it. Before he thought, his hand was buried in her hair, and he was pulling her down, closer to where he wanted her.

Then their lips met, and Luke sank into a world of sensation. So soft. So smooth. The taste of sugar and chocolate. Her lips parted. Tentatively her tongue swept against his and he was lost. Need exploded through his body, draining his control. He retreated, sucking in much-needed air.

Only then did he register that sweet palm still high on his thigh, just inches from where he wanted it. Avery seemed oblivious. "Are you okay?" she asked again.

"I swear, if you ask me that one more time, I'm going to flip you over and show you just how okay I am."

Just like that, the hand was gone. Damn shame, but probably for the best right now.

He'd veered onto a dangerous road tonight—led

astray by her inherent beauty and his own need for adventure—and he hadn't applied the brakes in time.

Knowing himself, he wasn't sure he could stop now. And his next crash might leave more damage than his last.

Six

If looks could kill, Luke Blackstone would be deader than a doornail.

He hadn't expected resistance to his appearance at the mill, since his brothers had already reestablished the Blackstone family presence. But with one look, Mark Zabinski had made his feelings toward Luke clear.

"I'm glad you came in, Luke," Jacob was saying. He turned back toward the employees in the office. "Everyone, I'm sure you know my brother Luke. He'll be joining us as a partner, so he wanted to take some time to learn more about operations."

The secretaries in the office smiled and welcomed him. The daytime shift manager shook his hand. The dagger look from Mark had been quickly suppressed, but a frown still lingered on a face already going soft around the edges. No one else seemed to notice.

Luckily, Aiden walked through the door just then. As he paused beside Jacob, Luke wanted to laugh. He'd never understood how those two could look so comfortable in their suits, even though Aiden still maintained a messy artistic style to his hair. Just the thought of wearing a suit jacket every day caused Luke's throat to start closing.

"Well, ladies, we don't want to keep you from your lunch," Jacob said, much to Luke's relief. He was ready to get the espionage part of his visit over, so he could see Avery.

He simply couldn't get her out of his brain. Her soft hair, silky skin and eager kiss. He had every intention of going to the therapy center this afternoon. No appointment. No reason for going…except for not being able to forget the taste of her tongue. Her sweetness flavored her, and had given Luke a contact sugar rush. He could tell himself he simply wanted to invite her out on an adventure, but deep down, he knew he was lying to himself.

"We do need to head out," Clara said softly. "I don't want to get caught in that bad weather coming in this afternoon."

"Oh, I think it will be this evening before that hits," Aiden said. "Y'all will be safely home before that."

"Most definitely," Jacob agreed. "We want everyone to be safe."

The significance of those words wasn't lost on Luke as he gave the ladies a quick goodbye, then followed his brothers out the door. What they were doing here today, and in the days to come, was about the safety of everyone involved with Blackstone Mills—both employees and family.

Still, Luke tried to keep it light. "Let's get on with this," he said, rubbing his hands together. "I've got places to be—"

"Places more important than this?"

Luke didn't care much for Mark's hard tone, so he slowly swiveled his head to stare at the man who had followed them out of the office. "As a matter of fact, yes. I have plans for Avery tonight." Only she didn't know it yet.

The flush that swept over Mark's jaw and neck was satisfying to Luke, even if it was petty of him.

"Let's head over to the manufacturing floor, then back this way," Jacob suggested.

"I'll catch up with you when you get to the accounting office," Mark said. "I need to check out a computer problem over there."

"Good deal," Jacob said on his way down the hall. "We need to go over the plans for the computer system in that department anyway."

Aiden and Jacob were gone in seconds, but Luke couldn't stop himself from looking back. He glimpsed Mark's face blazing with an inordinate amount of fury before the other man turned away, leaving Luke to wonder if he had pulled a tiger's tail with his needling remark.

He followed his brothers over to the manufacturing part of the plant, easily slipping into his public persona as he greeted acquaintances. He may not truly be joining the company as a full partner, but he cared about these people.

He'd do whatever was necessary to ensure their safety.

Dealing with people had always come easy to him. Until his accident, he'd been quite the extrovert. The dark period following his accident had birthed an extreme need for solitude. Slowly exposing himself to people again was going okay, as long as it wasn't a big crowd.

Today was working well for both purposes.

Talking with people in small groups of two or three, casually leaning on his cane and offering his TV-interview smile, allowed him to be accepted, to let down guards and to see what more familiar eyes might miss. After a couple of hours, he hadn't found anything suspicious. But at least they'd accomplished the first step: making his presence at the mill a natural occurrence.

For everyone except Mark, at least. Luke could still feel his resistance when they met up again near the accounting department. He knew things were about to get interesting when Jacob waved them on while he and Aiden talked over a problem with an employee.

The small accounting office was quiet. A lot of the employees had left early to prepare for bad weather. Being overly cautious, schools had let out early. Plus this tour had taken a bit longer than Luke had planned. He hoped to rush them through this last department so he could get over to Avery's before the thunderstorms started.

Mark made himself look busy fiddling with papers on one of the desks. Luke ignored the other man's aimless movements, his mind wandering to thoughts of what he would say to Avery.

Finally tired of the manager and all the noise he was making, Luke turned to face him. "What're you doing?"

"What do you mean?"

Mark's stiff shoulders and tight mouth gave Luke confirmation that Mark was gathering his courage for…something. Luke didn't have the patience to wait. "Why don't you just spit it out?"

His gaze slid away from Luke's, but Mark's chin jutted out in challenge. "I simply want to understand. I mean, why would you bother with Avery when before long you'll be heading back to fame and fortune? After all, it's not like she's your usual arm candy, is she?"

Luke didn't answer. He needed to get his temper under control first. Mark's words had a derogatory tone. Luke wasn't sure if it was directed toward Avery or himself. Neither would be appropriate.

His silence didn't impact Mark, who seemed to gain courage the more he talked. "It's okay. Somebody will be here to pick up the pieces after you *walk* away."

Again, Luke let the jab go, but he couldn't keep quiet. The more information he had, the more he could warn Avery. Well, that probably wouldn't go over well, but he'd figure out something. "You mean you?" He cocked his head to the side as if he were truly interested.

Mark just shrugged, grinning.

That lit Luke's fire. He was known to say stupid stuff before checking himself, and anger weakened his already tenuous control. He didn't often lash out, but when he did—ugly stuff. "If I understand gossip correctly, you and Avery have been dating for almost a year. Or rather, *had been* dating. If you had closed the deal before I got here, picking up the pieces wouldn't be an issue—but then again, I guess coming in second might be an experience you need."

Luke knew his arrogant grin topped Mark's smirk any day. Not that Avery had ever mentioned being upset over not seeing Mark romantically, if their dates had even been that. Besides, Luke would probably be the last person she'd talk with about Mark, but Mark didn't need to know.

"Tell Jacob I had to leave," Mark snapped.

Luke didn't manage to wait for Mark's office door to slam before he murmured, "If I feel like it, a-hole... which I won't."

Luke stared at the tight seal of the door for long moments, his frustration urging him to burst through and remind that jerk whose family was in charge here. But he didn't let himself move. Getting all up in Mark's grill would make him look jealous.

Just like Mark's overt comments had done for him.

Luke had nothing to prove. But that didn't stop him from wanting to.

"Mr. Hutchens, I want you to pay close attention to how you're feeling. Call me immediately if those muscles seize up again, instead of waiting until you can barely make it here. Got it?"

Avery gave the old man a stern stare, wishing she could just follow him home and watch him 24/7 to make sure he was okay. Or as okay as he could be with terminal pancreatic cancer.

"Are you bossing me around, missy?" His stare was a challenge all its own.

But Avery wasn't backing down. "You betcha."

"Well...all right." The fact that he retreated so quickly concerned her. Mr. Hutchens had been her patient for a while, and he liked to play the crotchety old dude when she gave him orders. But always playfully. He'd rather hurt himself before he hurt her.

If he wasn't playing the game today, he definitely wasn't feeling well. Of course, having your back muscles contract and not let go didn't feel so good, no matter what your other health issues were.

"Now, come in again tomorrow—"

"I can't afford that and you know it."

The bell over the door sounded as she glared at him. "You will come and you're not going to pay for it, either, so get over that pride of yours. I want to keep you upright and mobile. That's the goal." *For as long as I can.*

He gave a sage nod before glancing over her shoulder at the newcomer. "Well, I'll be. Lucas Renegade Blackstone. I haven't seen you since you went and got all famous." He grinned. "At least, not in person."

Avery breathed deep, almost able to feel Luke's gaze on her back. Unable to think of a delay, she reluctantly turned around to face him. Heat burned her cheeks as she remembered his kiss from the night before...and her response.

"Avery here working on you, too?" Mr. Hutchens asked.

"Sure is," Luke said, flashing a grin in her direction.

But not today. She'd have remembered if she had

an appointment for him on today's schedule, especially since they'd canceled the rest of the afternoon appointments for impending bad weather. So why was he here?

"She treating you right?" Luke asked, oblivious to her inner panic.

Mr. Hutchens stood a little taller, though Avery could tell by his quick breath that it hurt to do so. "Always," the older man said. "And how're the legs? I saw the footage on television. That wasn't a pretty wreck."

The practice footage had played on newscasts in their county for weeks following the accident, then again after Luke had been released from the hospital. Since he was a homegrown celebrity, everyone around Black Hills had devoured the slightest tidbits about his accident and recovery.

Avery studied Luke from under her lashes as the men talked sports. He leaned casually against his cane, as if it were an accessory instead of a necessity. While charming, he wasn't laying it on thick. His responses to whatever Mr. Hutchens said were genuinely warm. She'd seen that same sincerity on his face during television interviews. He was honestly interested in other people, which made him so much more darn appealing.

As if he needed any help with that.

"Would you do me a favor, Mr. Hutchens? As soon as my slave driver here clears me to get back behind the wheel, how about we go for a nice, fast drive?"

"Wow. I've never ridden in a really fast car. Reliable ones, yes, but never fast." And the twinkle in the older man's eyes told them just how exciting that would be for him.

"Well, I have a beaut. She drives smooth and steady—unless there's an operator error." Luke winked at the older man. "Don't worry. I'll be careful."

"I'm pretty sure you won't."

Avery laughed. Leave it to Mr. Hutchens to peg Luke so accurately.

"You laugh, young lady," Mr. Hutchens said, "but the truth is, when a chance comes once in a lifetime, you take it. And don't rely on the brakes or you'll regret it."

"Very sound advice," Luke agreed. He tilted his head in Avery's direction. "See? I'm right."

Ah, the polite male equivalent of *I told you so*.

"Mr. Hutchens," he said. "I'll be in touch."

"I see my daughter pulling up in the parking lot," Mr. Hutchens said. "And it's almost time for my medicine. I will see you tomorrow, missy."

"Yes, sir," she said, indulging in a quick hug.

"And you," he said, pinning Luke with a look, "you take good care of her, you hear?"

"Oh, I will, sir."

Was she reading an innuendo in Luke's reply that wasn't there? A flush swept up her neck and across her cheeks.

Maybe not, because Mr. Hutchens winked. "I can see she's in good hands. Good afternoon, son. Missy."

"Let me walk you out, Mr. Hutchens," Cindy said.

"Are you leaving now, too, girlie?"

"I'm hoping to get home before it pours," she said. "You sure you'll be okay, Avery?" she asked with a quick glance at Luke.

Avery appreciated the support, since her shaky insides were making her wish that her sassy receptionist would stick around for once. "Yeah," she said instead. "I'll get everything closed up." She ushered them to the door, eager to get any conversation over and done with. "Y'all be safe."

She and Luke stood side by side as they exited the door and walked slowly to Mr. Hutchens's daughter's car. The wind from the coming storm whipped at their clothes.

"What's the matter with him?" Luke finally asked in a low tone.

Avery matched it, though there wasn't anyone left to hear. "It's not a secret. Pancreatic cancer. Not too much longer now."

"Any insurance?"

"Yes, but therapy benefits can run out pretty quickly." Something that frustrated Avery to no end. Not because she needed money, but because it kept her patients from seeing her as often as they needed to.

Luke glanced across at her. "Why wouldn't you let him pay?"

"Because then he'd use not having enough money as an excuse to not show up." She shrugged. "I'm not really helping with the cancer anyway. Just trying to keep him as mobile as possible for as long as we can. Manage the pain a little. He's got a great attitude despite a terrible prognosis."

"That's wonderful, Avery...what you're doing."

She dismissed the compliment, because tooting her own horn wasn't ladylike. "Somebody needs to take care of them." And she'd been doing it all her life, right? That was her place. And her joy.

"I see."

She couldn't tell if he was agreeing with her statement or what, so she simply nodded. But his next words caught her attention.

"So who takes care of you?"

Her gaze shot to his, clashing with those amber eyes while the implications hit her hard. Who *did* take care of her? Who ever had? No one since she was a kid. At least, not that she could remember.

Uncomfortable exploring the question any deeper, she walked back toward the checkout counter. "I know you didn't have an appointment this afternoon. What do you need, Luke?"

"I'm here," he said with a charming grin, "because I thought it would be more fun to create mischief than be tortured."

She should have teased back, slipped into casual mode. But a flood of remembered sensations from the night before held her immobile.

Luke tried again. "I think it's time for another adventure."

Oh, Lord help her. "I don't think an adventure is a good idea."

Considering how much she wanted a repeat of yesterday's kiss—definitely not.

Would she even survive another? Between the fun and the fear of hurting him from last night, she wasn't sure her heart could take it.

Could it? "Definitely not a good idea."

Luke took her concern in stride. "It rarely is but that's what makes it fun. The danger."

Oh, it was dangerous all right. This was getting out of hand.

A taste, remember? Oh, yeah. She'd almost forgotten that little pep talk to herself—and she desperately wanted a taste like she'd had last night. But was she willing to put herself out there, to risk making herself vulnerable again to Lucas Blackstone, of all people? She tried to clear the tightness from her throat. "What did you have in mind?"

Luke didn't blink. "How about the drive-in? They always have something fun to see." He wiggled his eyebrows and grinned. "Something spooky, for good cuddling. And it won't be open too many more weekends before closing for the winter."

Before she could respond, the lights blinked out. Avery froze. Then the emergency lights clicked on, lending an eerie green glow to the room. Only then did Avery notice that the world outside had darkened to midnight and rain had started coming down in heavy drops.

"I don't think Cindy beat the rain home," she murmured.

"Nope," Luke said. "And neither will we."

Instantly alert, Avery walked to the window and searched the slope of the parking lot through the increasing sheets of rain. "Where's Nolen?"

Luke shifted beside her, his arm brushing hers. Such an innocent touch for such a sensual response deep inside.

"He didn't bring me. Aiden dropped me off and was gonna send Nolen back for me later."

Despite the gloom, she turned an incredulous eye

in his direction. "Have you not listened to the weather today?"

She saw a flash of his white teeth. "Guess I didn't think this through very well. But in my defense, having your brother wait while you ask a woman out is a bit awkward, if I could even convince him not to get out of the car."

Avery didn't have siblings, but she knew from observing others that a man's brothers were his first source of friendly ridicule. Aiden would never have stayed in the car. "Well, you won't be going anywhere anytime soon."

Luke stared out the front windows. Rain lashed at the asphalt so heavily as to obscure the view. An occasional glimpse of tree limbs dancing was all that made it through. "I see that," he said.

"No." She shook her head. "I mean, for longer than you think. Remember the bridge at the bottom of the hill?" They couldn't see it from here, but it was the only access to the facility drive. Avery's heart pounded as her brain kicked into overdrive. "It floods in heavy rains like these. That's why we canceled our afternoon appointments."

Luke moved closer to the window. "That quick, huh?"

"All the water from uphill flows back down here. It flash floods, so we take extra precautions." Including having a comfortable living space that allowed her to stay here cozy and safe—and usually alone.

"So this means we're stuck here—for the night?" Luke asked, a curious tone in his voice.

Avery swallowed hard, her mind on her fear of the storm and a new fear...of being cooped up with the sexiest man she knew…for hours on end. "Probably so."

"Well, that's an adventure by itself, right?"

Seven

"I need to lock everything down," Avery said. She stepped over to secure the front doors, then walked in the other direction, leaving Luke to stand there and twiddle his thumbs—a safe distance away.

Only he'd never been a twiddle-his-thumbs kind of guy. Following along to the workout room, he watched as she made sure all of the equipment was unplugged, including the computers. She was as thorough as he'd expected her to be—just as she was with her patients.

His meeting with Mr. Hutchens still haunted him. The elder man's stalwart attitude. Avery's careful attention to the man's needs and lack of concern for his wallet. Yet through it all, she'd approached the whole situation in a way that got the job done without attacking the man's pride.

A lot like she'd done with Luke. Guess all those years of studying others had paid off.

Just then, a rumble of thunder built outside, shaking the building until it ended in a crack. Avery's breath caught and she winced.

Luke realized something that he'd missed in all his years of knowing Avery: she definitely did not like storms.

As she finished securing the back door, she turned toward him. Her stiff back and wary look left him wondering if she thought he would pounce. Or was it just the weather?

"We can wait it out in my office, if you want," she said quietly.

He didn't really have a choice, and that made him inordinately glad.

He followed her down a short, windowless hallway by sound rather than sight, his cane plonking with every step. She disappeared to the left and he paused in the doorway. A few fumbling sounds, then a drawer closing, and an electric lantern flared to life.

Luke blinked to clear his vision, then found himself staring in surprise. This might be Avery's office, but it looked more like a plush, feminine version of the retreat Aiden had built for himself at Blackstone Manor. One corner was dominated by an antique desk with the expected accoutrements, but there the usual description of a doctor's office ended.

He couldn't tell what color the walls were, but it was warm even in the deep shadows. There was an armoire, which he suspected held a media system, and a deep upholstered couch that looked wide enough for him to sleep on—though not wide enough for them together.

Not that he should be thinking about that— Hell, who was he kidding?

Avery gestured toward the high-end furniture. "Make yourself at home. It's gonna be a while."

Seeming oblivious to him, she reached into the bottom of the armoire and pulled out a radio. She'd obviously used it before because it was tuned perfectly when she turned it on.

The announcer was moving quickly through a multitude of weather warnings and storm watches, including a flash flood warning for their county.

"No kidding," Avery muttered under her breath.

Luke could only grin. Avery often projected the image of being calm and in control—except in the face of two things: any form of sexual attention from a man and, from what he'd seen tonight, thunderstorms.

"This is really nice for an office," he said, hoping to soothe her nerves as he settled onto the couch.

She surveyed the space from behind her desk. He couldn't see clearly, but he was pretty sure she blushed.

"Well, I end up staying here overnight some due to weather, so I wanted it to be comfortable."

"Does this happen often?" he asked.

"I realize it's probably foreign to you," she said, shuffling the papers in front of her, "but some of us are afraid to drive in storms. And I can get caught here unexpectedly." She chuckled, though it sounded strained. "So it's less stressful than trying to get to my house since it's so far out of town."

"That sounds like a safe option to me," he said.

Her shoulders relaxed a bit, but she didn't look up. The papers were slowly migrated into a series of neat little piles. Then she began moving them to the nearby filing cabinet.

It couldn't be more obvious that she was uncomfortable having him here. Of course, she'd been on edge since that kiss last night—and he seemed to be making it worse rather than better.

On her next trip past him he leaned forward to reach for her. Her eyes widened, then she tried to sidestep and change direction just as his hand met her arm. A moment's push and pull, then she tumbled into his arms with a cry.

Unexpected, but oh so right.

Warm weight, softly honey scented and extra wiggly. Just like that, all the reasons he shouldn't touch her disappeared. Then a loud crash of thunder shook the building and Avery changed direction. Instead of pulling away, she dove in close, clutching at his shirt, burrowing against his chest.

The slight tremble in her hands brought his barriers down even more. His palms found the skin of her upper arms. Up and down, under her sleeves, he instinctively moved to comfort her—

Only comfort wasn't the result.

He'd wondered since meeting this adult version of Avery how she would feel against—and under—him. He had to admit it. But he couldn't have fantasized how perfect she would feel in his arms. Slowly his hand traveled up along her neck to her chin and lifted her face to his.

This kiss wasn't tentative, but Luke didn't rush.

As he leaned in, he breathed deep, soaking in her honey scent. Then his lips brushed over hers, coaxing her to open.

She signaled her surrender by melting against him. Soft flesh pressed to his chest. All he could do was pull her closer. Then his focus narrowed to the play of her tongue against his.

Avery twisted more fully toward him, their bodies meeting in a collision that had Luke seeing stars. The good kind.

Her hands fisted into his shirt and Luke shot straight into overdrive. He guided her legs over his until she straddled his lap, but their mouths never parted.

All that lovely pressure right where he wanted it. And he wanted *more* of it.

He pulled her hips tight against his groin while he sucked lightly at her bottom lip, then moved his lips back over her jawline to the sensitive column of her neck. He couldn't stop his hands from roaming, sneaking beneath her scrub shirt to finally cup the breasts he'd been fantasizing about all too often.

She moaned, arching her back to press into his palms. Only it wasn't nearly enough.

Something happened as he whisked the material over her head, because suddenly the silken mass of her hair swept down around them. Her scent flooded the air. Luke's heart raced, rivaling the speed of his favorite car.

His mouth migrated to the plump mounds now in reach. He squeezed with his hands, plumping them even more. Then he let go of his control, nibbling and sucking until she squirmed in his lap. Her nipples hardened. Her thighs tensed. Her cries filled his ears to the exclusion of all else.

She raised her arms, lifting her long hair up, then letting it sift through her fingers to cover her bare shoulders once more. Luke moaned. Avery's gaze swept down to his, her gorgeous irises now darkened in the glow of the lamp.

For a brief moment, sanity returned. Alarm bells sounded, reminding him how vulnerable she was, how caring.

But then she lowered her mouth to his once more and he could only feel. Not think.

Luke wasn't sure if it was five minutes or five hours later—all he knew was that some new sound had invaded their world of pounding rain, sighs and groans. It jangled along his nerves until he could no longer ignore its presence.

His phone.

Pulling back forced a protesting groan from deep in his throat, but his family might be worried. "Just a minute, baby," he murmured.

Digging the phone out of his pants pocket proved a challenge—one he didn't accomplish until the ring tone had silenced. But then it was too late.

The screen lit up in the dark with a missed-call message from "Aiden's wife."

The nickname he jokingly used to poke fun at Christina when she got too bossy cut through the haze of lust quicker than a hot knife through butter.

Luke's brain sped from zero to sixty. His brother Aiden had come home...and found a wife. His twin had come home...and found a family.

Luke had come home…and found himself making out with Black Hill's most eligible bachelorette.

This was not a pattern he wanted to follow.

He found himself acting on instinct rather than logic. The first part came easily: he lifted Avery from his lap and set her next to him on the couch. The second part, not so much. Not bothering to search for his cane, he forced himself upright by sheer will and limped to the door. Before slipping through, he turned back to the silent woman behind him.

"I'm sorry, Avery."

"I thought you were taking Avery to the drive-in tonight."

Luke turned from his solemn stare out the front parlor window to face Christina's question. "I am. Maybe. At least, I hope so."

Her dark, perfectly arched brows lifted. "Well," she demanded, "are you or aren't you?"

He wanted to tease her, but his nerves wouldn't let him. "I guess I'll find out when I get there."

"So…what did you do?"

The teasing grin came more easily to his lips than a confession. "What makes you think I did anything?"

"The crack in your confident veneer was my first clue."

Hmm…he should have known she was too smart for his own good. "I screwed up and she's probably mad at me."

"Let me guess—you aren't gonna let that stand in your way?"

He probably should. Holding Avery close had been the best thing to happen to him in a long time…

sweeter than he'd remembered from their first kiss. It was territory he shouldn't explore. Indulging himself wasn't fair to Avery when he wasn't sticking around for anything permanent.

So why was he going back to the therapy center just two days later? He shook his head. "I promised Avery I would help her have fun. This is just a little pothole, that's all."

"Good."

Now he raised a brow. Would she say the same thing if she knew what he'd really done? "Come again?"

"Avery needs someone who will help her get out of her own way. And you need someone who will demand a little more of you than looking pretty and driving fast."

"But—"

"Just work with what you have and see where it leads. After all, surprises are fun, too. Right?"

Christina's words rolled around in his brain as he made his way back to the kitchen. They made perfect sense. Except Luke still felt the dangerous desire to take his relationship with Avery further than friendship.

Surely they could go out on a public date without him giving in to temptation? They couldn't get in too much trouble in a parked car surrounded by people. Well, teenagers did, but they were grown adults. He could control himself...right? He ignored his misgivings by focusing on the task at hand. "Mary, you're a sweetheart for putting this together."

Luke had jumped on the chance to take a picnic snack pack on his date with Avery, instead of having to stand in line at the concessions stand. The thought of all those people made him feel like he was breaking out in hives. Besides, Mary made the best food.

He wanted a quiet night—just him and Avery watching a movie together in the back of her SUV. If she would even let him in the therapy center after his behavior night before last.

He had no idea whether she would welcome him with a forgiving smile or slam the door in his face— which was why he'd decided to spring this date on her at the end of her workday. She'd be less likely to make a scene, which would give him a chance to at least argue his side. And he'd have Cindy there to help plead his case…if Avery hadn't turned her against him yet.

He just wished he was picking her up instead of being driven there by Nolen. He hadn't been cleared to drive yet. The emasculating feeling would have come to any take-charge male, but for Luke, it was multiplied by his extreme need to be behind the wheel.

"What made you choose the drive-in for your date, Lucas?" Mary asked.

Luke grinned, letting her chatter push aside the self-doubt. Mary called all the boys by their given names. No nicknames for her. He could remember many a rainy afternoon he'd spent down here having cookies, warm right out of the oven. Sometimes alone. Sometimes with one or both of his brothers. But every time Mary used the cookies to bribe them into talking. About school, girls, their dreams, life.

She was a good woman. One who deserved all

Christina had gone through to ensure she and Nolen were taken care of for the rest of their lives.

"You remember how Avery's mother was," he said after swallowing.

Mary nodded. "Rumor was, she could be pretty strict."

"Yes, ma'am. Avery didn't get to do a lot of the normal hangout stuff the rest of us did. Formal events? Green light. Swimming in the creek or going bowling? Not so much. I thought this would be fun for her." But he hadn't thought the level of temptation through all the way.

"If anyone can show that girl how to have fun, it would be you. You always were off doing something more interesting than chores or schoolwork."

Luke grinned. "I tried."

"Y'all have fun." Mary winked. "But not too much fun. You'll be in public, after all."

"Since when has that ever stopped me?" Luke teased, flashing his trademark wicked grin. But after their night flooded in, Luke needed to be very careful. He fully intended to get them back on friendly ground. He liked Avery…a lot more than he should. But it wasn't fair to her to get sexually involved, then return to his normal life a whole state away.

They could still be friends, though, right?

So he lifted the basket, balancing it on the side opposite his cane, and walked out the back door to meet Nolen.

He distracted himself with thoughts of Avery. Too bad she was so darn cute when she got flustered. He couldn't resist teasing her. Any other woman might smile in invitation, look at him through her lashes, even lick her lips in response. Not Avery. She tripped over her own feet and dropped things. It amused him, but not in a condescending way. Almost as if he had to smile. His heart filled with happiness every time she stumbled, because that was her reaction to *him*.

The only frustrating part of this whole scenario was the fact that he would be sitting in the passenger seat, waiting to arrive. This wasn't his thing. *He* should be driving. *He* should be picking her up. When would his life return to normal? He might be able to cope with not racing, if he could just get behind the damn wheel again.

It wasn't just frustration. So much of his identity was wrapped up in racing that he felt like half a person when he couldn't do it. Half a man when he couldn't drive to a date.

No one else seemed to get that.

Luke stuffed his feelings of inadequacy down hard as he reached the car. But they popped back up to the surface over the littlest of things, like when Nolen took the basket and loaded it himself.

All these new, dark emotions were difficult for Luke to handle, a somber doppelgänger he wasn't used to facing. His biggest fear through all of this was that this new part of his personality would linger, dig deep into him, instead of letting him return to the easygoing, superficial star he'd been before.

But tonight wasn't about him. It was about helping Avery loosen up and have a good time. Though not too good a time—for either of them.

So he swallowed his pride and made his way to the passenger-side door, praying rejection wasn't waiting for him at the end of this ride.

Eight

Cindy's eyes widening was Avery's first clue that Luke had walked through the front door. Since he'd canceled his appointment for earlier today, she should have been surprised. Somehow she wasn't.

Luke didn't give up. He took things in stride and kept on truckin'. Avery wished she was capable of doing the same.

She smoothed her facial features to a careful neutral and prayed she would get through this first meeting post-humiliation as quickly as possible. After all, she was still his therapist. They needed to be able to be in the same room together for her to help him recover—though she had no idea how she would touch him again without remembering how it felt to have her hands moving on his body with passion. Or how it felt to have his hands on her.

She glanced nervously at Cindy. She hadn't told the other woman what had happened. Somehow it was too personal, too private to share even with one of her best friends. Eventually…but not today.

She cleared her throat and tried to take control of this situation. "I'm sorry, Luke. I don't have any more appointment times this afternoon. We're closing."

"But we could—" Cindy halted when Avery shot a glance full of daggers in her direction.

"Not a problem, since I'm not here for an appointment," he said.

Avery's head swam at his words.

"I thought we'd try that drive-in date."

Her mind went blank. "Why?"

"It's Friday." He grinned, charming and carefree. Her complete opposite. "It'll be fun. You deserve some downtime after this week, don't you?"

That sounded well and good, but why was he really doing this? Before he'd left the office the other morning, he'd babbled a whole speech about wanting to still be friends, but she hadn't been buying it. No sexy, charming man like Luke had ever wanted to just be her "friend."

"She's overthinking it." Cindy had to add her two cents' worth.

"I am not."

He and Cindy just stared at her in silence.

"Okay, I usually am." She simply didn't know how to stop.

Luke didn't have the same problem. "Don't think. Just do."

Easy for him to say. But she had promised herself a taste— of freedom, of passion, of Luke. *Stop hem-*

ming and hawing and do it. She should just take what little she could get.

After all, it could be fun. The old-fashioned drive-in theater on the north side of Black Hills had never been on Avery's radar. She loved movies, actually— but in the comfort of her own home. Of course, other than the drive-in, there was only a two-screen theater in the Black Hills square. And it mostly featured kids' movies and oldies.

The drive-in usually showed current movies. The double features were pretty popular, especially in the summer, when families could go for a kid-friendly movie first, then the adults would watch the more mature movies after laying the kids down to sleep in their cars. So she'd be in public, which should keep her from giving in to all the exciting tingles Luke inspired.

Or maybe not. After all, she'd be in a parked car. In the dark. With Luke.

Stop analyzing. Just do it. "Okay. Want me to drive?"

Luke frowned, none too happy about that, but still nodded his head slowly. "Yeah, that will be easiest." Then he snapped back to happy Luke. "I've brought everything we will need."

Cindy chuckled, sparking Avery's irritation. "You planned ahead?"

"Yep."

"What if I had said no?" Avery asked.

This time, Avery's assistant didn't restrain herself to just laughing. She said, "An inexperienced girl like you is not gonna turn down a chance to make out at the drive-in."

Ouch! Avery couldn't even look at Luke. Instead

she glared across the counter. She must have been at least a little frightening, because her friend grimaced and walked back into the equipment room.

Turning her attention to Luke, Avery startled when she found him up close and personal. Within-kissing-distance close. Something she couldn't stop noticing.

"I wasn't trying to insult you," he said.

"Um, okay." What was she supposed to say?

"Really, I wasn't." He tilted his head to the side. Probably to see her better, but Avery couldn't help thinking it was the perfect angle for kissing. Man, he'd tasted so good.

"I know your parents didn't let you do a lot of the same stuff the rest of us did as teenagers. Especially after your dad died," he said. "I just thought this would be one of those things you don't have any experience with…and I could give you that."

Oh Lordy, was he for real?

"That's very sweet of you, Luke."

"I'm not doing it to be sweet. I have my own ulterior motives."

Finally he leaned in, brushing his lips against her cheek. Compared to the other night, the step down in passion was almost an insult. Her skepticism must have shown on her face, so he tried again.

"Listen, you're the first thing that's gotten my heart racing in a long time. I think that's worth exploring, don't you? Yes, I let things get out of hand the other night, and that's not fair to you. I'm sorry."

At least this humiliation wasn't public. Luke could never know how far she'd wanted to go the other night. Especially since it was obvious he didn't feel the same.

"So what do you say?" he asked.

"I'm all about a new experience." Even if it wasn't the one she really wanted to have with Luke.

Apparently not being able to drive was going to be an ongoing irritation for him. Avery pulled the car around and Nolen loaded it. Standing around waiting did not come naturally to Luke.

He swallowed his pride and made his way to the passenger-side door, reminding himself he should be grateful just to be alive. Avery lowered the hatch back, the basket safely stowed inside, then grinned at him as she climbed into the driver's seat.

That smile was infectious, as was the excitement behind it. Like a kid in a candy store—and he intended to feed her all the sweets she could eat tonight.

"What's in the basket?" she asked.

"It's a surprise from Mary."

"Chocolate chip cookies?"

"Good guess, but I'm not telling. You'll have to wait and see."

Her full lips turned into a plump pout, but the excitement practically sparkled in her eyes. So she liked surprises. As much as he liked giving them.

He tried not to think of the ways he could use this to his advantage—and for her satisfaction. That could be dangerously addictive.

Trying to get his mind back on track, Luke directed Avery on where to enter the theater grounds, purchase tickets and choose one of the rows. As she started to pull into one of the slots next to an old-school microphone stand, he stopped her. "Reverse it."

She froze with her hands properly held in the ten-

and two-o'clock positions on the steering wheel. "What?"

"Back in—so we can climb in the rear and watch from there." He grinned at her startled look. She really hadn't been to a drive-in theater. "Just trust me."

"Um, I don't back up very well." Her look met his under her raised brows. "Would you do it?"

The lump in his throat was hard to swallow down, embarrassingly so. "I thought I wasn't allowed to drive."

"I'm hoping you won't be driving over the speed limit here, which is, what? Five miles an hour?" She grinned. "Don't think you can do much damage going that fast, can you?"

As he rounded the car and slid behind the wheel, the slight shake in his hands left Luke disconcerted. Avery waited outside as he shifted the car into Reverse and smoothly backed it in with minute precision. He sat for a moment, savoring the feel of the wheel in his hands, the hum of the vehicle beneath him, and ached for what he couldn't have.

Yet. Not if he wanted to heal properly. Some days it didn't seem worth the wait, but he wanted his lower body to work the rest of his life.

So he forced himself to wait it out, not risk the pressure a sudden accident might put on his healing bones. Not long ago, he'd have trusted in his skills to avoid an accident. Now doubt had set in.

Avery's gentle knock on the window pulled Luke from his thoughts. He stepped out of the car. "See, easy."

"Show-off."

"I can't help that I have skills." He winked, officially leaving his melancholy behind. Then he opened the hatch. Propping his cane against the bumper, he started to arrange the back area of her car to his satisfaction. Finally he turned to her. "Climb in."

With a bemused look she did, then inched her way toward the basket.

"Oh, no you don't," Luke said with a chuckle. "No peeking until I say."

Again with the lovely pout. Those lips might just be the biggest temptation he'd ever faced.

He got the speaker box set up in the corner, then maneuvered himself into the car. The back gate was designed so he could close the hatch, but leave the pop-out window lifted to view the screen. Perfect. The warmth from Avery's body soaked into his skin as he settled next to her. Had any race ever felt this dangerous?

"And this is why we sit in the back," he said after clearing his throat. "Much more comfortable."

"I see." Avery's voice sounded breathy.

Good. His considerable ache left him needing to know that she was affected by him, too.

Opening the basket, he pulled out the softest blanket he'd been able to find at Blackstone Manor and draped it over them. The heat multiplied beneath the barrier between them and the cooling autumn air.

"Um, Luke?" That breathlessness had strengthened.

He couldn't force himself away—not even an inch. "Yes?"

"Is this, um, what you're supposed to do at the drive-in?"

"Yes." *Oh, yes.*

"No wonder my mother never let me come here."

He grinned, then pulled the basket over to him once more to unearth the goodies inside.

Around them the lot filled with cars. There was lots of chattering as their neighbors got ready for the movies to start. First an older release about a group of kids hunting for treasure, then a current thriller sequel for the adults. Luke had gotten them there early so they could settle in without being recognized.

He'd forgotten what a social event this was for most people. Big groups of teenagers would congregate down front during the first movie, then retire to their cars for necking during the second. Families spent time visiting with other families, and during the summer there would be lines of blankets on the ground with supper picnics.

He'd forgotten all about that, because frankly making out had been more interesting as a teenager.

But inside their little cocoon, snuggled beneath a blanket that thankfully disguised just how much he was enjoying this, they would avoid the crowd. Even though he knew he shouldn't—Luke wanted Avery all to himself. He pulled out the popcorn and offered her a choice of pouches. "Caramel, cinnamon sugar or ranch?"

She smiled. "Miss Mary knows I love cinnamon sugar anything."

So that's why the housekeeper had insisted on that flavor. "Try this." He opened the bag and pulled out a couple of popped kernels encased in a brown syrupy coating. She tried to reach up with her fingers, but he was having none of that. Catching her gaze, he eased the food forward until he breached her lips.

Their gazes connected as she glanced up in question; she never looked away. The pleasure that spread over her face lit him up inside.

"Good?" he asked.

"Mmm-hmm," she murmured, still chewing.

Intrigued, he fed her again, and again, the last time brushing his fingertips along the seam of her lips. He barely caught the shiver that snuck over her. Then he licked his fingertips clean of the sweet coating. "Delicious."

"Wanna try some?" she whispered.

He wondered if she realized the invitation that displayed so prominently in her eyes. He'd guess not, but that was one of the things that drew him. No overt invitations, no cookie-cutter come-ons…just Avery. He bet she was the sweetest, hottest thing he was ever going to taste.

What better time than now?

Just as he leaned in, her eyes widened. That quick guilt snuck in. It was an unfamiliar emotion. Luke lived his life full throttle. Regret was rare. But he needed to remember that giving Avery mixed signals wasn't fair to either of them. A good woman like her deserved better than a player like him.

So instead he tried to ignore the softness of her breasts brushing against his arm, the warmth of her thigh alongside his and the way his spirit sang with the sensations that declared his body was alive.

He couldn't stop thinking about her kiss. If he took her lips now, they would be soft as butter, sweet with sugar and hungry for him. He just knew it.

Luke pulled back and held up another piece of popcorn. The glaze over her eyes kept them from focusing, urging him to push his boundaries, but he held himself back.

Like prolonged foreplay. The best kind.

Luke gripped the blanket in his fist to keep from pushing for more. The night was dark, with barely any moon. But they weren't teenagers to be caught in a lip-lock by all the kids running by. As a matter of fact, as he glanced out at the end credits rolling up the screen, he noticed people slowing as they walked past the car.

At least no one had pressed their face to the window yet.

Finally Avery reached across him for one of the popcorn bags, the quick press of her softness against him a jolt to his senses. Then she leaned back and started to munch on her own, leaving him chilled. The cocoon of sensation they'd been lost in for the last hour and a half turned cold.

"I think you've been spotted," she mumbled.

"Meaning?" he asked, though he knew the answer already. In the periphery of his view he could see people gathering. Like the rapid building of a mob, the group grew in numbers as they murmured among themselves.

"People know you're here. You know how small towns are... They love a homegrown celebrity."

Right now, Luke felt like a celebrity for all the wrong reasons. The last thing he wanted was to be on display.

"Oh, dear."

"What?" he asked.

"I believe the mayor just joined them."

Dang it. Just like that, his vision for how this evening would go disappeared—replaced by a steady stream of people who would probably go on and on about his accident. Talk about a downer.

Tonight was about Avery, not the hometown celebrity. More than having fun or even having sex, he wanted to shake the foundations of her safe world. He couldn't do it with an audience. And having the crowd to come to him would only put her in the public spotlight right alongside him.

He sighed, throwing the blanket aside. Playing the gentleman role, as he had two times in three days, was not nearly as rewarding as people made it out to be.

Within minutes of Luke scooting out of the car, the real estate between them and the next row became a revolving door of people. Avery couldn't even see the bottom half of the screen because of the crowd. She huddled into the shadows of her car, shoving popcorn in her mouth like a squirrel storing for winter, not willing to risk the exposure. She recognized more than a few patients, members of their families, and knew her business would be a hotbed of gossip if she set one foot near Luke. Maybe they'd forget the car he'd come from.

Between Luke's teasing challenge back at her office and her desire to save face in front of Cindy, Avery hadn't given herself time to think this decision through. She and Luke couldn't just go out as friends. All eyes would be searching for the slightest behavior that proved they were more than that. She loved these people. That didn't always mean living with them was easy.

She'd lived all her life under their scrutiny, and

tried to avoid it when she could. But it was the constant questions and insinuations that would be thrown at her after Luke left town that she was truly trying to avoid.

As the second set of movie credits rolled, Avery put the leftover food back into the basket. The last thing to be packed was the blanket, fluffy and soft. Heat rolled over her as she remembered those few precious moments with Luke wrapped tight against her. Would she have survived four hours of that? Maybe not, but it would have been fun to try.

Thirty minutes later, she couldn't help wondering if more time under that blanket would have meant driving them both back to her house at top speed, instead of turning onto the highway that led out to Blackstone Manor. Which one did she really want?

The quivery feeling in the pit of her stomach told Avery she wasn't sure. And to her disappointment, Luke had made his position quite clear: friends, not lovers. Now he remained silent, probably exhausted from the overload of people. Her guilt over leaving him to handle himself alone weighed her down, but self-preservation was a strong instinct.

Luke leaned against his car door, staring out the window at the farmland flashing past as they left the lights of Black Hills proper.

His voice bordered on surly when he finally spoke. "Why didn't you remind me what a social event the drive-in could be?"

"Um, I've never been. Remember?"

"I just remember making out with my girlfriends," he grumbled. "Tonight wasn't what I had in mind."

Just what Avery needed. A reminder of times past

and all the women Luke had had better experiences with. "It wasn't my fault. You could have stayed in the car."

"But you didn't go out of your way to help, either, did you?"

Her face flamed. "I didn't know you needed my help." After all, he was the big star. Though honestly, she had taken the coward's way out.

"You could have joined me." He turned back toward the window. "Or were you just too embarrassed to be seen with an old, broken-down celebrity?"

Uh-oh. "It wasn't that at all." She struggled to gather her thoughts while still concentrating on the road. "I just—"

"Didn't want to be seen with me?"

This was going from bad to worse. Tonight hadn't been a dream date, but now it was turning into a nightmare. Why couldn't these things ever go right for her?

"Me staying away had nothing to do with not wanting to be seen with you, or your injuries. I work with people with mobility issues every day. What have I ever done to make you think I would be ashamed of you?"

He didn't answer, but continued to stare out the window. The silence that filled the car seemed heavy with recriminations—something Avery couldn't handle. And she couldn't leave him thinking that she was embarrassed by him in some way.

"Yes, I did choose to stay away. But you have to remember, Luke—one day you'll leave. And I'll be the one left behind, dealing with their pity." She gestured between them, wishing she could see his face.

"Whether anything happens between us or not, they'll think it did." *And that I wasn't good enough to keep you here.*

The continued silence forced more words out.

"I'm sorry if that's selfish, but I don't know if I can handle that."

When he didn't respond, a glimmer of something hot sparked deep in her belly. It grew with every second he didn't speak until she recognized the anger building inside her. There he was, sulking like a spoiled boy, when she'd done nothing but protect herself, her reputation. How dare he?

Finally reaching her limit, she whipped over into a church parking lot—one of the few buildings out here in the boonies. She gave a soft growl. "I can't talk about this and drive."

"I can."

It took a moment before the flash of realization came. That's what was happening. She shoved the gearshift into Park and turned on him. "Is this about the driving? Luke, you are not broken. Not doing it right now is a protection for your body, not an indication that you are anything less than you were. You will get there. It takes time."

At first, she thought he'd continue with his silence. Instead he spoke, his voice rough with emotion.

"This just... None of it is right. I should have picked you up. I should have set up the car and made you comfortable. I should be the one protecting you, not you having to protect yourself. It's just—wrong." He shoved his fingers through his thick hair. "I feel powerless. Every day." He glanced her way in the dark. "Except when I'm with you."

She swallowed hard.

"When I'm playing with you, challenging you, kissing you, all that other stuff melts away. Until I wish you were by my side for—" His touch was firm as he pulled her close. "Why am I picking a fight when there are much more pleasurable ways to remember I'm alive?"

Whatever she'd been thinking disappeared beneath the onslaught of sensations as his lips devoured hers. Here there was no self-consciousness, no fear of being seen and judged. Only her and Luke. His body and hers. And the magic he made her feel.

His hands tilted her head to the side so his lips could cover hers fully. His tongue pressed inside, brooking no argument. Her body thrilled at his invasion. Without thought, her hands went to his biceps, pulling him closer. He sucked on her lower lip, leaving her mouth full and swollen. Then those wicked lips trailed across her jawline and down the curve to her neck.

His soft mouth contrasted with the light scrape of his teeth against her skin, sending shivers across every inch of her body. She heard herself moan as he found the pulse point at the base of her neck. His harsh breath as he devoured her. A knock at the window.

Wait—what?

Jerking her head to the side, Avery saw a stream of light coming through the car window across the dash, then up Luke's body. She pushed him away. "Oh Lord, no."

Luke blinked. "What's wrong?" She laid her palm against his cheek and turned his head so he'd see the light.

Another knock sounded on his window.

"I can't catch a break tonight," he mumbled. With what sounded suspiciously like a chuckle, Luke straightened up and pressed the button to roll down his window. He didn't seem concerned that a sheriff's deputy stood outside, having clearly caught them in a compromising situation.

This was even more embarrassing than if they'd been caught at the drive-in. No, she had to get caught in a church parking lot. Heaven forbid!

"Everything okay, folks?" the deputy asked. Avery suspected she heard amusement in his voice.

"Oh, not by a long shot," Luke replied.

Lordy, they were going to jail if he kept that attitude up—and he was certainly in the mood to push it. "Luke, stop it." She leaned forward. "Everything's fine, sir. We're just going."

"Might want to. You be careful behind the wheel, Miss Prescott."

When he said her name, something clicked. Avery realized the dark figure outside the car was none other than Douglass Holloway—an officer she'd done some rehab with. As he walked away, Avery wondered how long it would take Deputy Holloway to relay exactly what he'd seen Avery and Luke doing at the church.

Nine

Avery slowed her jog down to a walk as the end of the wooded trail behind her house came into view. She'd hoped some exercise this Saturday morning would take her mind off last night's fiasco, but she continued to replay the officer's amusement in her mind. After twelve hours, her cheeks were permanently stained red.

She'd gotten the impression that Luke had been secretly laughing at her as she'd primly driven him home and dropped him off. Not surprising. He could laugh something like that away. He hadn't spent his entire life going on date after date where embarrassment was the main course. That was probably why she'd let the casual relationship with Mark go on as long as it had—no attraction meant no accidents, no tripping and no flying food.

And no pulse-pounding, muscle-gripping excitement, either.

Avery paused, bending to rest her hands on her knees while she breathed deep. After she'd left Luke in the drive without a word last night, she had a feeling all her excitement was over.

Her muscles now heavy with fatigue and recrimination, Avery continued down the trail until she reached the edge of the woods along the east side of her house. One of the reasons she hadn't wanted to move closer to town had been the land surrounding her family's home. The three-story house was way too big for one woman, but the thirty acres it sat on fed her need for privacy and nature—something hard to find closer to town.

She squinted as she moved from the cool shade of the woods into the bright sunlight. Walking across the side yard gave her a clear view of the drive that circled the front. To her surprise, the black Bentley that Nolen drove for the Blackstones idled in the drive. Great. Now she wasn't just embarrassed, she would have to face Luke sweaty, messy *and* embarrassed. Nice.

She diverted from the side door around to the front. Luke was navigating the stairs as she reached the porch. With a small wave and smile for Nolen, she climbed to the long veranda that ran the entire length of the front of the house. She couldn't help running her hand nervously over her damp hair.

"Whatchya doing here this morning?" she asked, a little breathless, a lot peeved. Maybe by avoiding eye contact she could keep from tripping over her own feet and tumbling off the edge of the porch.

A trip to the ER would just be icing on this week's cake.

Silence surrounded them for long moments, then she heard the thump of Luke's cane as he moved

closer. Out of the corner of her eye she saw him approach, hand outstretched, until his fingers found her
chin. Gentle pressure insisted she raise her gaze to
his. Only then did he speak.

"I think I owe you breakfast after the way I acted
last night. Would you go with me?"

Why did those amber eyes have to look so sincere?

She shook her head, trying to resist. "I don't think
it's a good idea, Luke. Maybe we should just let it go."

His look darkened. "I don't want to let you go. I
wasn't kidding when I said being around you makes
me feel alive, cuts out all the noise."

"So this is all about you?"

She felt like a heel for saying it out loud, but she
needed to know. He was already shaking his head.

"You know it isn't. I told you we needed to have
fun, shake up the boundaries. Are you giving up so
soon?"

"As you can tell, my track record is horrible. Last
night was a disaster."

"But memorable. Right?"

"Yeah, I haven't been able to get Deputy Holloway's face off my mind all morning."

Luke laughed. "Look at it this way—you livened
up his probably boring shift." His thumb rubbed along
her cheekbone. "Breakfast. Please."

She shouldn't. She knew she shouldn't. She wasn't
the type of woman to do casual relationships. But
deep down inside, she wanted just a little more of
him—even if she had to suffer humiliation to get it.

With a sigh and careful steps, she led him inside.
After a quick shower and change, she almost defiantly
met him back in the front parlor. He'd shown up at

the last minute. She wasn't decking out in makeup and pearls. He'd have to settle for jeans and a comfortable T-shirt.

He stood in front of the mantel covered in pictures of her mother, father and herself. The reminders of her family made her both happy and sad, but she tried to hold on to the happy part.

"I'm ready."

Luke picked up a silver-framed picture of her parents smiling at the camera, arms wrapped around each other. "Do you have any other family around here?" he asked.

"No." Avery swallowed against the lump forming in her throat. "Both my parents were only children. I was an only child. There may be some distant cousins, but no one close."

"Even after my dad died, and Mom's car accident, I've always had my brothers. We may give each other grief, but they're there, you know?"

"I've got friends," she said, hating the defensive note in her voice. Her family had meant a lot to her, but she'd known long before her mother died that they would one day be gone and she'd be alone. "I'm not isolated. I'm active in the community."

"You don't get lonely?"

"Of course. Doesn't everybody?" She shrugged. "But I'm surrounded by people all day, people I genuinely care about. That counts."

"Good."

His approval shouldn't make her glow inside. She'd shaped her life into what made *her* happy, or as close as she could get without outside interference. Though she'd love to have a family of her own, her life was full without one.

Luke didn't seem in any hurry to head out. "You've never wanted to leave? Move somewhere else? Start over?"

"There are people who need me here. I can't just abandon them." So she hadn't realized how entrenched she would become once she started on this path, but she cared too much about the people in Black Hills to leave them high and dry. She tried to shrug her doubts away. "Besides, where would I go? There's no reason for me to be somewhere else."

"I just can't imagine being content in one place. Just signing the lease on my apartment made me itchy."

And she was pretty sure he had no plans to hang around here. *Don't forget that, girl.*

She'd rather not dwell on it now. "So what was that about breakfast?"

Snagging her hand as if afraid she would change her mind, Luke led her out to the car, where Nolen patiently waited. Luke waved the butler aside and helped her into the back of the car. Nolen slid behind the wheel. They were on the road in minutes, the smooth purr of the Bentley slowly soothing her nerves.

Avery held herself stiff, back to prim and proper after her lapse the night before. Luke obviously didn't feel the same way. He leaned in close, his tempting mouth inches from her ear. "Interested in a repeat of last night?"

Would he run screaming if she said yes?

She couldn't stop the shiver that raced over her.

She also couldn't stop her glance in Nolen's direction. "Shh," she warned.

Luke's laughter told her he found her reticence highly amusing. "It can't be worse than being caught by the cops."

The red flush Avery thought she had washed away in the shower returned full force—and burned until they reached the restaurant fifteen minutes later.

The Wooden Spoon had been serving Black Hills for almost half a century, and was still one of the best places to eat. Breakfast was particularly popular, and seating was at a premium despite three dining rooms full of tables and counter seating. Still, Luke swept past the hostess stand with his wicked smile firmly in place. One of the girls trailed behind them like a groupie until they reached a back booth, where she set their menus on the table with a shy smile before backing away.

"How'd you manage this?" Avery asked.

Luke was already perusing the selection, oblivious to the magic he'd just worked. "Call-ahead seating," he said, giving her a quick wink.

Deadly, that's what that wink was to Avery. Able to get around every last barrier she built, no matter how solid. She turned to her own menu to avoid any more Lucas Blackstone charms.

"Guess you got perks like this all the time in North Carolina, huh?" she asked.

Luke shrugged. "Some."

A waitress appeared. Much older than the hostess, she handled waiting on a celebrity with a calm friendliness and efficiency that left Avery grateful.

Avery doctored her coffee with flavored vanilla creamer—her sweet morning indulgence. "Do you miss it?"

"North Carolina?"

"Yes." Avery glanced sideways at him. "You've lived there quite a while." Yet he hadn't put down any roots at all. Only what was necessary.

Luke took a sip of his own coffee, black and sweet. "The place? No. The racing? The track? My crew? You bet."

"Why?"

His look of surprise made her a little sad. Had no one ever asked about this before?

"It's thrilling, for one. I control the vehicle and use it to conquer whatever obstacles appear before me."

She could see how that would appeal to Luke.

The Blackstone brothers had spent their childhood after moving in with their grandfather James, without control over anything. Not their father's workaholic hours, which he kept in an attempt to appease his father-in-law, and not his death at the mill. Their mother had been unwilling to stand up to her father, especially after becoming dependent on him. And the constant arguing between James and Aiden Blackstone—the rebel brother who hadn't backed down over anything, including leaving home without any prospects because he couldn't live with James one minute longer.

Escape. It had become a habit for Luke. She'd watched him, had seen him work off his frustrations and anger with speed. Sometimes it had been scary, but it had worked. Most people would think Luke was the calm Blackstone brother. Oh, no. He had the same turbulent emotions; he simply handled them in a different way. Aiden raged against authority. Jacob became the authority. Luke simply drove.

"Most of all," he continued, "while I'm behind the wheel, I don't think of anything else. Nothing but the road and my next move."

The intensity, the passion in his expression rolled over her. This wasn't a guy on an ego trip. He wasn't in it for the money and the fame. Luke loved being in a car—no wonder the thought of waiting out an entire season had been immediately rejected. How tortuous was it for him to watch from the sidelines?

"It's the same with you."

Avery glanced up to find Luke's gaze tight on her face. "What?"

"It's the same when I'm with you." He reached out and ran his thumb back and forth across her bottom lip, leaving her all melty inside. "When we're together, all the buzz just stops. No more static."

Her heart almost caved in. She wanted to warn him not to say things like that, that she might get attached. But then the waitress appeared with plates loaded with fluffy omelets, stacked pancakes and crisp bacon. The smell commanded Avery's attention. Her stomach growled. "Good thing I ran this morning," she said.

He turned away from the pancakes he'd been eagerly cutting to brush back her hair, which was still damp around the edges. The feel of his skin against her cheek and ear had her breath catching in her throat. "Honey, calories are the last thing you need to worry about."

Oh Lordy, this man was dangerous—and he knew it, too. "Are you trying to butter me up?"

He swallowed his mouthful of food, then grinned. "I figured I better after last night. I'm not usually such an ass."

That much was true. Luke might speak impulsively, but he rarely lost his temper or let much push him into a bad mood. Last night had been an anomaly. Yet looking back over all Luke had been through, it wasn't surprising.

She'd been off her game, too. Dating wasn't a normal situation for her. Luke wasn't a normal guy for her.

Lifting the maple syrup, she toasted him with the bottle. "Well, if your apologies include pancakes, I'll always accept them."

To her surprise, he didn't laugh her off, but met her gaze with his own clear amber one. The darker flecks in his eyes became visible as he leaned closer, then closer still. Avery's heart thumped against her chest. Was he going to—

She quickly inhaled, afraid to pull away, but afraid not to. Then came the scent of coffee, syrup and man as Luke brushed his lips over hers. Warmth against warmth. Like a sugar rush, the thrill raced straight through her. Too quickly it was gone.

"Dammit, Avery, I'm sorry."

Reality returned, and Avery automatically glanced around to see if anyone had noticed the kiss. One nosy busybody and half the town would have her married off to him in an hour. Wouldn't that be a great gossip storm after he left town again? With her right at the center of it all, and him nowhere to be found.

Mark's brown gaze studied Luke, then flared with a dark, fiery emotion almost akin to hatred. At least, she thought it was. He quickly shuttered his expression and turned back to the man beside him, talking quietly.

Was he jealous of the kiss? She hadn't thought he would be, after all, he'd only ever initiated a few end-of-the-night brushes across her cheek. He'd never really pushed for more. Theirs was a casual, convenient relationship that benefited them both on numerous social occasions. Or so she'd thought...

Avery couldn't worry about Mark for long.

She turned to face Luke, almost afraid of what she'd see in his expression. "What?"

"You tried to explain to me last night why it would be hard for you if people assumed things." He dipped his head for an instant, reminding her of a much younger Luke. His words were hesitant. "I wasn't really in the mood to listen, but I did understand. Yet here I am, not twenty-four hours later, stepping all over that boundary once again. So... I'm sorry."

Avery realized she stood on a precipice, looking over the edge into unknown territory. Darkness loomed, scary and uncertain. The landing would definitely hurt. But wouldn't she kick herself one day if she held back now?

The past week had been a roller coaster of emotions. Making the most of their time together wasn't as easy as it should be. Too many emotions were coming to the surface. Along with physical needs that she'd allowed to lie dormant for a long time—too long. Maybe she wasn't built for casual, but she simply couldn't walk away from this chance to be with Luke. However he wanted.

"No, Luke," she said, then swallowed hard. "I'm sorry. I was only thinking about myself, and not how my actions would affect you." She thought about Mark's glare, and imagined the pitying looks she'd receive after Luke left. Somehow, she knew they wouldn't carry the same weight after having Luke's lips on hers.

"Let's just play it by ear, okay?"

Luke's brows shot up. "What? Avery Prescott without a plan or set of rules?"

"You keep it up and you're gonna owe me another breakfast…" she warned. He just laughed. And deep inside, Avery knew she'd made the right choice.

If only her decision hadn't been challenged quite so soon.

Just as they finished breakfast, a shadow dimmed their booth. Glancing up, Avery was horrified to see the deputy from the night before. Instinctively her body crowded into Luke's, as if he could shield her from the embarrassment, even as she told herself there was nothing to be embarrassed over.

The deputy grinned. "Morning, folks," he said.

Luke nodded, reaching out to shake hands. "Morning, Deputy Holloway. How are you?"

"Fine. Fine." He shook his head slightly, adopting an expression of mock concern. "I'm just glad to see you folks made it out this morning…after your late night."

A choking sound escaped Avery—one she wished she had held back. The burn had returned to her cheeks, but Luke just laughed once more.

The deputy winked at her. "Well, enjoy the rest of your day."

As he walked away, he stopped here and there to talk to several people—including a few who frequented the diner every morning to share gossip. Avery could almost see the story of their midnight encounter spreading across the room in the whispers and grins. By the time Luke had paid and they rose to leave, it seemed like all eyes were on them.

As they made their way out, the whispering seemed to follow them in a wave, until one voice rang out. "Y'all behave now."

Well, at least she wasn't paranoid.

Luke gave a salute without stopping. Even the hostesses whispered as they approached the doors, only to stop abruptly as they walked by.

"Y'all have a good morning," one said with a sly smile.

Luke just smiled back and continued to guide Avery out with the support of his hand at the small of her back. Nolen's black car was just coming up the road.

"Well, I guess it's official now," Luke said.

She cut her gaze at him, confused. "What is?"

"Us."

Her heart pounded. Maybe she wasn't as ready as she'd thought. "I'm sure it will all die down."

"I doubt it. I screwed up, so you have no choice but to date me now."

Do you want me to? "How's that?"

"You wouldn't want to make me the laughingstock of Black Hills by rejecting me, would you?"

"That's totally not how the story would go." *She'd* be the laughingstock. Probably still would be after he left. Why couldn't two adults just have some fun together without the small-town gossips automatically assuming forever after?

"Oh, Avery, you should know by now that I'm always right. That's why you should just let me have my way."

Even if his way was dangerous to her?

"Regardless," he said, "you just did your good deed for the day."

That stopped her in her tracks. "What?" Luke was talking in circles now.

"Just think how many existences you're livening up with that story. You're doing your civic duty to entertain others."

"Only a man would look at it that way."

"Honey, in a town this small, that's the God's honest truth."

Almost a week later, Luke wished more than anything that he was back in that diner with Avery. Or anywhere with Avery.

As Nolen pulled the car into the parking lot of the local playground, Luke almost had a full-body cramp. The place was covered in people.

And not just locals. Luke only recognized about one in every four faces. Deep down, stage fright set in.

How the hell had this happened?

A year ago, seeing this crowd would have had his energy and excitement skyrocketing, but not today. All he could think about was the weakness in his legs, his cane…and that Avery wasn't here with him. What if he fell? What if his legs buckled?

Locals actually knew Luke Blackstone, the person. They'd understand. These other people were here to see Luke Blackstone, racing celebrity. That was a whole different ball game, one he hadn't faced since his crash.

He'd done one press conference after his release from the hospital. After that, he'd stuck to phone interviews and private meetings. He'd prefer the world see him whole rather than broken. Just another reason to push for his return. If he never had another case of nerves, he'd die a happy man. Which made him more sympathetic to what Avery had endured for years in order to date at all.

As he stepped from the car, Christina must have read his thoughts. "I'm so sorry, Luke," she said as she rushed to his side.

"How'd this happen?" he mumbled, nodding in the direction of the crowd. "I thought this was supposed to be me with a few kids on the playground." He caught a glimpse of something out of the corner of his eye. "Is that a news crew?"

His brother appeared behind his wife.

"What the hell, Aiden?" Luke struggled to control his breathing.

Christina's big brown eyes filled with tears. "I'm so sorry, Luke."

Aiden spoke over her shoulder. "One of the board of trustees members leaked it to the university newspaper, thinking it would be great press for the fundraising efforts." He shook his head. "It just spread from there."

And Luke hadn't heard a word. He'd stopped watching the news after his accident, afraid he'd catch a story about himself and risk seeing the footage from his crash. Even now, he could barely watch the sports stations. Though he forced himself to stay up-to-date on the racing circuit, it was hard. Harder than he'd like to admit.

Sucking in a deep breath, he forced himself into the professional persona he'd cultivated over the years. For once, the identity didn't slip on as easily as before. Like an ill-fitting coat, it pushed and pulled against him, making him uncomfortable and unusually grouchy. If only Avery were here, he'd have just a touch of the calm she usually possessed. But she'd probably hate this kind of thing. She was more a one-on-one kind of girl.

"Well, this looks interesting…"

Luke glanced over his shoulder to see those blue eyes lifting shyly to meet his and he wanted to kiss her. But he wouldn't, because despite what she might think, embarrassing her in front of large groups of people wasn't his goal. Instead, he let his voice soften with welcome. "Hey."

"Hey, yourself." She glanced around and he could see the uncertainty as it clouded her fine features. "I thought you could use a little support. Maybe."

"Definitely."

Suddenly handling himself in front of this crowd didn't seem quite so hard.

"Maybe you should work the crowd a little and give a short interview to the news crew first," Avery suggested. "That will make it easier to move them back behind the barricades so y'all can shoot the commercial."

"Avery, that's a great idea. Thank you," Christina breathed. Aiden patted his wife's shoulder, then called a few men over to get things organized.

By the time Luke had shaken several hands and signed a bunch of autographs, he felt more in control. Avery was beside him at first, but it wasn't long before the crowd edged her away. He kept her in his peripheral vision, but he didn't really need to. It was as if his body could feel the distance between them.

Finally he stopped and found her with his gaze. Perhaps reading his thoughts, she pushed through until she once again breached the circle Aiden and several other men had formed around him to help with crowd control. After that, he kept her close, refusing to take more than a few steps without catching her hand.

How she felt about this, he wasn't sure. Somehow, he didn't care. In his selfishness, he simply knew he needed her. And in that moment, he vowed to break through the very boundaries he'd put in place. Tonight.

When he was being interviewed, she wasn't far away. He let himself talk as if talking to her, and deep inside he relaxed. This feeling was dangerous, but he was too intoxicated with her presence to care. He'd worry later—when he had no other choice but to return to the life he'd built before her.

Though he was tired after, Luke realized how right Avery had been. Now that he'd made his rounds, the crowd willingly moved back behind the barricades so they could watch without interrupting. And Luke felt much more comfortable than he had when he'd arrived. If he felt a touch of trepidation as he looked over at the half dozen kids starring in the commercial with him, he sure as hell wasn't gonna show it.

Avery walked over to the director and spoke quietly. After his nod, she came back and took his hand. "Follow me."

It didn't take him long to realize she was leading him over to the kids. He kept his persona firmly in place. "Hey, guys," he said as they approached the group.

He got a few "hi"s back, a couple of giggles and some shy smiles. If he wasn't mistaken, the kids were just as nervous as he was.

Then Avery spoke. "Kiddios, I want you to meet a friend of mine. This is Luke, as y'all know. Luke, this is Steven, Mariah…"

He tried to grab on to the names and not let them escape into thin air, but he'd simply met too many people today and his brain refused to cooperate. But he wouldn't let that stop him.

Crouching down as best he could, he brought himself to the kids' levels. They looked between five and ten or so—not that he knew a lot about telling kids' ages. But they were cute. A set of twin girls with ringlet curls. A boy in a local softball club jersey. An older girl with a bright blue cast on her arm. Two other boys, one with crutches and another with a walker.

"Luke is a friend of mine," Avery said. "And he's nervous about being in front of the camera."

Luke felt his feathers ruffle until she went on. "Y'all can help him out, right?"

As the kids started throwing out their best child-size advice, Luke realized she'd started a dialogue he could handle that was still kid-friendly, making it really easy for him to be involved. In that moment, something happened. Luke wasn't sure what, but he knew he'd never find anyone like Avery, who helped him so selflessly, looking out only for his comfort and caring about whether he succeeded or not. Yes, they'd had some fun together, but it hadn't been just him giving to her. It had been mutual.

How incredibly lucky was he to have that?

Without further thought, he grasped her hand and pulled her close. The feel of her body against his was even better than he remembered. He savored it.

Tilting his head down to hers, he murmured, "Thank you," then took her lips in a solid kiss.

Not a brush. Not a quick peck. His lips met hers without hesitation. He soaked up the feel of her, the scent and taste of her, until his body went haywire. Only then did he pull back.

His gaze met hers. He was lost in the world between them, until a sound shattered the bubble.

He looked to the side to see the audience of kids and a few grinning moms. "Ooohhhh," the kids cooed at them. Then all of them laughed. Luke couldn't help but join in. To his relief, so did Avery.

This wasn't just about sex. He wanted to do so much for Avery, big and little, just like she was doing for him. But he also wanted to take her to bed, and he had a feeling that experience would be completely different from the ones he'd had with other women.

Dangerous, but after all, he lived for the thrill.

He couldn't help but reach out and brush his thumb over the round of her cheek as she smiled, softly stating his need, his purpose. Their gazes met once more, his conveying a promise.

Tonight, she would be his.

Ten

As the crowd once more pushed her to the edge, Avery gave up fighting the flow. Weariness muted her purpose. Luke was holding his own, and she didn't want to feel like a groupie. Instead she turned in the opposite direction, finding an empty park bench to rest.

Only a few minutes passed before Christina sat down next to her. Avery could almost feel the questions before her friend asked them.

"That was some kiss," Christina started.

Avery took a deep, deep breath as her chest threatened to constrict. "Yes, it was." Part of her wanted to turn away, to not talk about this now...if ever. But avoiding it wasn't an option. That look from Luke earlier told her everything was about to change. Her body softened, anticipating that look becoming action. Even while her heart beat in fear for the future.

"Are you gonna be okay, Avery?"

Avery appreciated that her friend wasn't pushing for details. Christina spoke from concern, not from prurient curiosity.

"I'm not sure." She searched for words. "Luke's the most exciting thing that's ever happened to me. Has always been, from the time I was a kid."

Christina chuckled. "Yeah, the Blackstone brothers do have a tendency to be larger than life."

"What if I can't meet that?" Avery met her friend's concerned gaze. "I've always felt a step behind when it comes to Luke. The only place I'm in control is as his therapist."

"The woman I saw today wasn't just a therapist."

"I wanted to help."

"Because you care about him?"

"I have since we were just kids. Every day I'm with him, it only gets worse." *Dang it.* Avery swallowed hard, choking on the words that would reveal just how deeply she'd fallen. "One day he's gonna leave. I'll never be enough to keep him here…and everyone knows it."

Christina's cool hand enveloped hers, squeezing in sympathy. "Oh, honey, I know exactly how that feels. And I know that not everyone's story is going to turn out like mine."

They were quiet for long moments. With each second that ticked by, Avery's heart grew more uncertain. She, more than anyone, knew how devastated Christina had been when she'd thought Aiden would return to New York for good. Could Avery go through that herself and have her spirit still survive? "I'm not sure I can live through losing someone else."

"And you shouldn't have to," Christina said quietly. "But the alternative is never letting anyone close to you again. I think it's a little late for that with Luke."

Very true. Avery knew it, but acting on it, opening herself up beyond this point, was still scary. Could she live with the pain later? At least then she'd have the memories. Could she live with the emptiness of never having those memories at all?

Christina spoke again. "Do you really want to spend your time caring if everybody thinks you weren't good enough for him later? Or would you rather focus on whether he thinks you're good enough for him right now?" She squeezed Avery's hand, flooding Avery's senses with sympathy. "He's a great guy. I promise he's not just playing with you."

Avery knew that. Though Luke was often playful, he was also genuine. She had a feeling his ambivalence up to this point had stemmed from the fact that he truly did see her as a friend. Hard as that was for her to believe.

For right now, he needed her. Wanted her. Could that be enough?

In the distance, he stood so tall, so proud. But she remembered that moment earlier when he'd needed her. Her chance to meet him more than halfway, without being model perfect or fast-lane ready. "I want him," she murmured.

"Then take him," Christina said, "and prove to him he can't live without you."

Avery doubted Luke would ever see her that way. Racing, he needed. Avery was just a bonus during the off-season. But she couldn't live that way forever. And just like that, the lightbulb went on.

Hadn't Luke been trying to teach her to live in the moment? Have fun right now, without worrying about what anyone else thought or said? And wasn't she doing just the opposite by letting gossip and giggles and other people's judgments make her decisions for her?

"Boy, am I slow." She shook her head. "I can't believe how afraid I've been all this time."

"Been there, done that," Christina agreed. "Do you want to continue that way?"

Hell, no. Avery was ready to live on her own terms. She'd known this for a while. Now she had to quit dragging her feet.

When Luke finally approached, she stood alone, more sure than she'd ever been. He met her with a tired smile.

Her nerves skittering around inside her, she drew in a deep breath. "I sent Nolen home."

She'd expected a smart remark or a sexy wink. Instead his amber gaze held hers, some of that exhaustion melting away. He traced her cheek with his thumb. The explosions under her skin were deeper this time. Instead of fighting them, she let them flow over her.

Luke's voice was low, intimate. "I guess you're stuck with me then."

"Maybe I could give you a ride," she teased.

"Your place or mine?"

Her heart picked up speed, beating hard inside her chest. "Mine?"

He nodded, his grin a mixture of relief and anticipation. "Sounds like a plan."

God, she hoped so. As he took her hand and

walked to the car, none of the tension from the night of the drive-in spoiled the mood. Instead arousal built with every stroke of his fingers over the back of her hand. He continued to touch her on the ride home, but she couldn't decide if that was a good thing or not.

The closer they got to her house, the more worry set in. What if she didn't please him? It wasn't like she had a world of experience, though she wasn't a virgin. Logically, she knew how to make him feel good. But would she remember all that when the time came? Or would her body just go haywire and cause her to do something stupid?

By the time they reached her house, she was a bundle of nerves. Sure enough, she stumbled over the threshold and bumbled a few of the stairs. From behind, she felt Luke's hand grasp her own, slowing her to match his careful pace. They finished the climb to the second floor together. His touch calmed her down and ramped her nerves up at the same time. Please, don't let her mess this up.

Luke paused just inside the door to her bedroom, taking everything in with a sweeping glance. She wondered what he thought. Never having been a particularly girlie girl, there wasn't a lot of lace or pink in her room. The curtains were a floral print in soft yellows, blues and purples. She'd repainted a few years ago, covering the lavender of her childhood with a contemporary smoky blue. A darker version of the same colors graced the bed, complementing the blond wood furniture.

"Come here," Luke said, pulling her toward the bed.

This is it. How she wished she could shut off the

thoughts racing through her brain. They distracted
her as Luke propped his cane against the headboard
and shrugged out of his jacket and button-down shirt.
She allowed her gaze to soak in the muscles she'd
learned so well. But there wasn't long to enjoy the
view before he came toward her. Without a word he
slipped off her cardigan sweater, leaving her in a silky
tank top and khakis.

Guiding her to sit on the side of the bed, he eased
off her slip-on shoes. She scrunched up her toes, feeling naked. Exposed. But Luke was having none of
that. His strong hands enveloped one foot, his fingers
digging into the arch and pushing back to stretch her
calf muscles. Her moan erupted into the silence, her
brain registering a level of heaven she didn't usually
experience.

He glanced up, his eyes alight with sparks that
made her shiver. "Feel good?"

"How could it not?"

He just grinned and moved to the other foot. When
he finally made her stand again, she wondered if her
feet would support her. Shaky, but she wasn't in danger of embarrassing herself. Good thing, because
those wicked fingers went straight for the button of
her pants. Her tummy muscles twitched at the brush
of his knuckles. He didn't look up this time. Instead
he concentrated until her pants lay around her ankles
and her tank had sailed across the room to drape casually off the side of her cheval mirror.

Luke regained his feet with a push of his hands
on the bed. At the last minute she pressed her lips
together to keep herself from praising him. They
weren't at therapy. The fact that she was his physical

therapist was the last thing she wanted him to think about right now. Although that intent gaze trained on her bare middle was not the most comfortable thing in the world for her to focus on, either.

But he didn't rush. He soaked her in with his gaze for long moments before he picked her up and laid her on the bed.

She made a sound of protest, but he met it with a firm look. "Hush," he said. "I lift way more than your body weight at the gym every day."

He was right. And at least she hadn't tripped and tumbled into bed like she would have on her own. Curling on her side, she watched as he efficiently stripped down to a sexy pair of boxer briefs. A quick glimpse of the scars on his legs reminded her how incredible he was, how far he'd come...

Then he slid into the bed, and pulled the light comforter up against the chill in the room.

He crawled over her until she lay flat on her back with his body hovering above hers. He eased down tentatively, as if afraid his weight would be too much for her. He covered half of her body, his face buried against her neck. His erection cradled against her hip, one bent leg spreading her open without resistance. His rough thigh applied pressure to that most sensitive spot, urging her to lift her hips against him.

Perfect alignment. Automatically, her body melted, reveling in his heat and the weight that anchored her in this moment.

"What are you doing?" she whispered.

"Just relax," he murmured into her hair. "Let me soak you in."

For long moments, she couldn't let go. But then her

breath changed to match his. In. Out. Slowly deepening. His warmth softened her. His mellow scent
enveloped her.

Then his thumb moved along the left side of her
collarbone, his forearm brushing the cup of her bra.
How could such a slight touch feel better than any
other man touching her...ever?

"Just relax," he said again. "Just enjoy."

But she wasn't sure how she was supposed to relax
with his hands on her. He traced her collarbone out
to her shoulder. Then he explored the hollow right
below, and stroked down the length of her arm several times. Arousal built so quickly inside she broke
out in a sheen of sweat.

He moved back up the sensitive skin on the inside
of her arm before he traced the outline of her bra.
That touch, so close, but not quite enough, was pure
torture. She moaned, her hips twisting.

"There you go."

His voice, thick and husky, played heavily on her
nerves. She dragged her eyes open, wondering if the
emotion was real. His gaze followed the path of his
hand, but he didn't study her with abstract interest.
No, he was engrossed, just as he'd said. Utterly absorbed, his body hardened against her hip, speaking
without words what she needed to know.

Her restless body urged her to move. Luke's knee
kept her legs from closing, so she reached up with her
free hand to test the stubble that had barely emerged
along his jawline. He leaned into her touch like a cat,
powerful and soft. She traveled along the side of his
face to bury into his thick, sandy hair.

His heavy-lidded gaze lifted to hers, the connection complete. He rose so his mouth covered hers. His wicked hand splayed across her ribs, then meandered down to cup her hip bone.

His tongue breached her lips. His fingers tightened with lovely pressure. Avery's body drowned in sensation overload. Her hand tightened of its own accord, pulling at Luke's hair. He groaned, deep and long, as his body pushed against her, riding her through the smooth cotton of his briefs.

If she didn't have him inside her, soon, she might just explode without him—which was completely unacceptable. She twisted her head to free her mouth. Her hips lifted against his commanding thigh. "Luke," she gasped. "Luke, please."

"Just a little more, baby," he said against her skin, prompting goose bumps. "I haven't sampled all of you, yet."

That just might kill her, but at least she'd die happy.

Luke struggled to breathe deep, praying he could hold out a few more minutes. The intoxication of having Avery beneath him was a thrill not to be cut short.

Her skin brushed his fingers, soft as silk. As classy as Avery was, she'd be made of nothing less. But she wasn't passive—oh no, her hand in his hair conveyed her need without words. The sting of her pull complemented his sharp spikes of desire until he became one long pulse of need. She didn't just lie there like a pretty princess, but invited him inside with every lift of her hips and clutch of her hand.

Luke was surprised by the slight tremor in his hand as he reached for the front clasp of her bra. He'd always been wholly in control. With Avery, he felt anything but. His body demanded he ease the burning fever beneath his skin. More than that, he wanted Avery to feel the burning fever right alongside him.

He wanted it all, her all, until she'd never be complete without him again.

He didn't know why, didn't care.

Propping himself up on his elbow gave him a front-row seat to the reveal of a lifetime. His eager palms brushed the material back, revealing creamy mounds that shook with each breath she took. Awed with a kind of reverence he'd never felt before, Luke buried his face deep into the cleft between her breasts and breathed in her essence.

From his first drive, Luke had become one with his car, with that desire to eat up the ground until freedom burst over him. Now he wanted that same feeling—and he wanted Avery to share it with him.

Her rose-colored nipple felt smooth against his tongue, but quickly hardened beneath his touch. Both her hands now buried in his hair, she pulled him closer. Her body shifted and moved as if enticing him to ease the need inside her.

Yes. Oh, yes.

But it wasn't until those hands buried beneath the waistband of his briefs that he knew he'd succeeded. Unable to pull himself away from those perfect mounds, he continued to kiss her breasts as he peeled the material off. Avery's silky panties didn't fare as well. One hard pull and the barrier shredded.

It wasn't until his body was poised between her thighs that reality intruded. "Nooo," he moaned.

"What?" Eyes widening, Avery looked down between them. "Um, what's wrong?"

The last thing he wanted was for her to worry, but an afternoon spent with kids wouldn't let him ignore the obvious. "I don't have a condom."

"Oh." She collapsed back against the pillows with a giggle.

He glared. The raging state of his body did not find this situation the least bit funny.

One look at his face sobered her right up. She pointed to the bedside table. "Top drawer."

That he hadn't expected. After all, Avery didn't date much. Wait, had she and Mark—? Luke swallowed hard. This was not going according to plan.

But the unopened box in the top drawer said if Avery had been planning for visitors, they'd never shown up. He opened it and flicked a single package between his fingers. "What are you doing with these? Huh?"

Her cheeks deepened to a darker shade of red than they'd already been. "Wishful thinking?" she murmured.

Only Avery would be embarrassed by that. "I'm glad one of us was planning ahead."

"I wouldn't thank me yet. You might want to check for an expiration date first."

Determined to pay the little hellion back for teasing him, Luke quickly sheathed himself, then buried his face into the crook of her neck. Blowing against her skin had her squealing and squirming. Before long, he couldn't resist anymore.

Long sucking kisses moved him down her body to the sensitive spot above the joint of her hip. There he slowed, brushing his lips back and forth over the soft,

soft skin. The spicy scent of her arousal coated his senses. All he knew then was the need to please her.

Firm hands spread her wide, giving her no chance to hide from him. The slick, sensitive skin between her thighs reminded Luke vividly of the essence of Avery herself. So vulnerable. Yet strong.

Bending close he greeted her with a kiss. Then he opened his mouth, and proceeded to drive her crazy. Her moans and screams were music to his ears, mixing with the pounding in his blood to create a barometer measuring just how much pressure they could each take.

Finally her body pulsed one last time, her thighs tensing around his head. Instead of a scream, air trapped inside her throat, choking off the noise, ramping up the sensations. Only when her body melted into the bed and her breath released with a soft sigh did Luke rise up.

Looking across her loose limbs, sweat-slickened skin and shaking ribs, he knew he was seeing the real Avery. The woman behind the fears. The woman behind the nerves. The woman who'd got the orgasm she deserved. And he was the man who'd given it to her.

All those primitive sensations rolled around inside him, forcing him closer and closer. Lifting one of her legs, he made a place for himself between her thighs.

Her body resisted at first so he teased her with tiny strokes, then a little more. Just a little more, until she relaxed deep inside.

Like a spent battery recharging, her body regained vitality. Her hips shifted, tilting toward him, urging him deeper.

He clenched his fists in the sheet above her shoul-

ders, desperately trying to hold out. But once his hips
met hers, those primitive instincts could not be de-
nied. Especially not while looking down at her gorgeous face.

As his body pounded into hers, their gazes met,
desperately clinging to one another as if the meaning of life could be found in the other person. All too
soon, their bodies betrayed them. Avery arched into
him, bowing under waves of pleasure.

Her muscles tightened around him, the pressure
perfect. Thrusting deep, he opened up full throttle.
Heart racing, head pounding, he found the ultimate
high in the arms of the woman he'd never expected
to find.

In the following calm, Luke forced air into his
lungs, becoming aware of his suddenly shaking arms.
Easing over to the side, he settled next to Avery before he fell on her. But he couldn't stop touching her,
couldn't break the connection. His palm settled easily against the slight rise where each set of ribs met.
His hand moved up and down as she breathed, their
heartbeats slowing. Energy dissipating into the shadows darkening the room.

What was this unnatural need, this feeling inside
of Luke that screamed for him not to move too far
away?

Despite the warning signals flashing in his brain,
Luke had every intention of listening to his instincts.
He forced himself to walk to the attached bathroom
and clean up. After he'd made Avery comfortable, too,
he lay next to her in the bed and pulled her against
him in a reversal of their earlier positions. He smiled
at her limp lack of resistance. Though he knew im-

mediately when awareness kicked in, because her muscles grew taut one by one.

"Rest with me," he murmured.

"Clothes?" Obviously her brain wasn't on board yet, because full sentences weren't an option for her.

No way was he letting fabric rest between him and all the delicious skin tempting him to fully wake back up. "Not tonight."

"Too tired?" she whispered.

"Oh, yeah," he said, teasing a little. "I have a physical therapist who tried to kill me today."

Her giggle made him smile, even as it trailed off into even, peaceful breaths. Luke let the world fall away, until all that remained was the warmth between them and the feeling of perfection deep inside.

Eleven

Avery came to awareness by degrees, her body awakening like a closed flower to the sun, one petal at a time.

A soft light filtered between the part in the curtains—not quite full daylight. She felt the unusual warmth in her little cocoon of covers—enough to keep her sleepy. And the heavy weight of someone at her back… Had anything ever felt so heavenly? The core of her body throbbed as she remembered just who it was in bed with her.

Lucas Blackstone.

Gone were the girlish dreams from so long ago, fiercely replaced by the desires of a woman. She should feel shy, nervous about seeing him again this morning. After all, she hadn't woken up with anyone of the male species since college. And never with a specimen of Luke's caliber. Boys compared to a man.

But she feared she'd experienced far more than Luke's physical prowess last night. Touching him, savoring him, sleeping beside him… Her heart was long gone. Maybe it had been since she'd been a child. That hero worship from afar had blossomed to full maturity with time and space. But now—well, now there was no turning back.

Worried that her restless thoughts would cause her to move and wake up Luke, Avery eased out of the bed and stood for a moment in the cool air. Her naked body shivered—she wasn't sure if it was the chill or her surprise at actually being bare. But as she watched Luke reach out to find the warm spot her body had just left behind, curling toward it, she yearned to be beneath his hands once more.

But after such a long day yesterday, she imagined he'd want a hot cup of coffee this morning.

She quickly pulled on some yoga pants and an oversize T-shirt, then eased out the door before pulling it closed. He'd slept soundly all night with barely any movement. From his remarks at the center, she'd gotten the impression that wasn't common for him. She'd let him sleep…while she figured out how to act natural.

A cup of creamed coffee only served to remind her she hadn't had dinner last night. A protein bar steadied her jitters. The front bell rang as she was looking through the cabinets, wondering what she should cook for breakfast.

She hurried down the hall and into the front foyer, hoping to catch the visitor before the bell rang out again. The sound wouldn't be as loud upstairs—she knew from experience—but she wasn't sure how light of a sleeper Luke was.

With only that thought in mind, she threw the door open to find Mark standing on her doorstep. She froze. He hadn't been to her house for several months. She certainly hadn't been expecting him this morning. "Um, hi," she said with awkward hesitation, her mind still on the man sleeping in her bed upstairs. "What can I do for you?"

The classically handsome man frowned, a crease forming in his perfect brow. "You can stop talking to me like I'm a traveling salesman, for one. We've been friends a long time, Avery. Aren't you going to at least invite me in?"

She bristled at his tone, but good manners dictated she let him in to find out what he wanted. After all, her house wasn't on the way to anywhere. He'd come here for a reason. What that was, well, she couldn't imagine.

"I'm sorry," she said, stepping back and gesturing him inside. "I haven't been up long. My wits haven't kicked in yet."

She led him into the front parlor, pausing awkwardly next to the proper antique sofa that had belonged to her father's parents. As she glanced around, she realized this entire room would easily fit in at a museum. It still had the original fabric wall coverings from when the house had been built, along with needlepoint from her great-grandmother's own hand and original furniture. She'd made it into a sort of memorial to her family. Though it wasn't comfortable for lounging, she came here often to look at the pictures on the mantel.

Just as Luke had last week, Mark paced in front of the fireplace, studying the photographs she'd framed in antique picture frames to fit the room's decor. Mark seemed to fit here—he'd been born into one of the oldest families in Black Hills outside of the founding family, the Blackstones. He'd attended the only private school in the area, same as Avery. Had gone on to a prestigious college, and had done well as far as she could tell. He'd worked his way up into executive management at the mill, though "worked up" sounded a little harder than it had actually been. He'd never actually worked on the mill floor. He'd simply held white-collar jobs there.

Mark was an intellectual kind of guy—not into sports or cars. He'd filled his own house with antiques, liked the challenge of numbers and enjoyed fine dining.

"Would you like some coffee?" she asked.

Mark turned to face her, but his gaze wandered around the room, not landing anywhere for long. "I didn't come here for pleasantries, Avery. I came to ask if you think you're making the right choices."

That forced a double take. "What?"

He shook his head, as if he were talking to a disappointing child. "Avery, I saw you with him that other day, then yesterday. Do you really think this is the best thing for you? The right thing?"

Avery felt a wave of heat roll over her as she remembered meeting Mark's gaze in the diner. For a moment, she felt ashamed, knowing she had assumed she'd be good enough for a superstar personality like Luke.

His earnest brown gaze finally met hers. "You're

a small-town girl, a quiet homebody. Do you really think you can compete with his career? The attention? The freedom? The women?"

A familiar sense of inadequacy sparked deep inside Avery, spreading until her hands trembled. She knew if she took one step forward, she'd fall. If she picked up something, she'd drop it.

Instead she lowered her eyelids, wishing she could hide away from that knowing look on Mark's face. But in the darkness behind her closed lids, the sensations from the night before surfaced to flood over her. Her body moving in harmony with Luke's.

There'd been no shame last night. No clumsiness. Just two people exploring each other and giving each other pleasure. Luke may not love her, but they were friends. He wouldn't want her to be embarrassed by what they'd done.

"Mark, I appreciate your concern. But what happens between me and Luke isn't any of your business."

"We dated for a long time. Doesn't that count for anything?"

Therein lay tricky ground. "We went to community functions together. That's not dating." But that wasn't the whole of it. "You've been my friend for a lot longer than that, Mark. That counts for a whole lot more than a few appearances. If you have something helpful to say to me, great. But I will not let you make me feel inferior, simply to make yourself feel better."

A look of almost desperation came over Mark's face, furrowing his brow and glittering in his eyes. He stepped forward, grabbing her shoulders and shaking them a little harder than she liked. "I thought we were perfect for each other, Avery. You'd be an excellent hostess, a beautiful companion. We were meant for each other."

That was so not what she'd expected. "Mark, you never acted like you felt that way." She swallowed hard, wishing she didn't have to hurt her friend on top of everything else. "I'm sorry, so sorry if you wanted something more than friendship, but I've never had romantic feelings for you."

Mark's color deepened from red to purple. "So you think a small-town girl can compete with the excitement to be had in North Carolina?"

Ouch. "There's no competition."

"There will be...the minute he steps out of Black Hills."

He wasn't telling her something she didn't already know. "That's not your concern. Or mine, either." If she worried about the future, she'd go crazy. "I'm sorry that you learned exactly what was going on like this, but I never meant to hurt you."

"So you'd rather whore it up for one of the Blackstone brothers than be the lady your parents wanted you to be?" His hands squeezed, the pressure making her wince. "You could have been my wife, one of the most prominent women in Black Hills. Why would you ruin everything for him?"

Her gasp sounded loud in the room, but she didn't have long to dwell on the shock.

"That's enough."

Luke's voice rang through the downstairs, strong and clear. Mark let go of her, turning toward the entryway. The sounds told her Luke was coming down the stairs, though she couldn't see him from her angle.

But she could tell from the widening of Mark's eyes that he had a clear view of Luke's approach.

Avery looked back at the doorway just as Luke crossed the threshold, and she almost choked. It was Luke, all right. All gleaming muscles, in nothing but a pair of boxer briefs. Obviously, self-consciousness wasn't an issue for him.

From Mark's apoplexy, it was clearly an issue on his part.

As he took in all of Luke's bare skin, then turned to study Avery's loose-fitting clothes, knowledge dawned in his eyes. Uncomfortably aware of her bra-less state, Avery crossed her arms over her torso, only to realize the move probably made her lack of undergarments even more obvious.

Suddenly Mark twisted his lips into a smirk. "Well, well. You aren't just planning to whore it up... you already have."

"I said, that's enough," Luke said, the hard edge to his voice making Avery just a little bit scared, even though it wasn't aimed at her.

Mark's expression said the wheels were still turning in his brain. His gaze was no longer blank as he looked between her and Luke. The knowledge of the night they'd spent together added fuel to his earlier anger. He opened his mouth to speak, but Luke beat him to it.

"If you walk out right now, we'll just chalk this up to your disappointment in losing the girl." He crossed the room and placed a protective arm around Avery's shoulders. Her lashes fell for a moment as his fingers brushed over a sore spot from Mark's hold. Luke went on, "If not, I'll see to it that Jacob hears every detail.

And you can look forward to Monday being your last day at Blackstone Mills."

"You aren't my manager," Mark growled. "You can't do that."

This time it was Luke's turn to smirk. "No, but he can. And I'll make sure he does."

"Fine."

Mark stalked over to the door, and for once, Avery was glad to see him go. She didn't need people in her life who intended to tear her apart. Life had taught her that long ago.

Mark opened the door, then glanced back at where they stood in the entryway to the front parlor. Avery felt the large span of Luke's palm blanket the small of her back. Mark's gaze flicked down, then back up to her face. "Think about it," he said. The door slammed behind him.

Luke moved as if to follow, but Avery grabbed his arm.

Thankfully, Luke pulled her close. She rested her forehead against his chest, breathing in the musky scent of his skin. His hand covered the back of her head, holding her close until her trembling stopped. Then she forced herself to pull back, stand up tall and smooth down her hair—no matter how she felt inside.

"I'm sorry," she said, unable to meet his gaze…or anything else on him, for that matter. "I don't know what got into him."

"I don't, either," Luke said. "That didn't seem like jealousy. It was all aimed at you."

Avery was already shaking her head. "I didn't give him any reason to think that I—"

"I know," he assured her as he stepped closer.

There was no getting around the sight of all that sexy bare skin with him two inches away.

Skin she wanted to touch. Just as she had last night.

"What we do here is between you and me. No one else. Don't let him change that, okay?"

"I won't."

As he led her back up to bed, she was determined to hold on to that promise with all her heart.

"Master Luke, there's someone at the door for you."

Luke looked up from the racing magazine he'd been reading to find Nolen in the entryway to the front parlor. "Who is it?" he asked.

For once, the butler's somber face gave way to a slight smile. "Someone I believe you will want to see."

Luke glanced across at his brothers, who were playing a game of chess near the fireplace. They both shrugged.

Guess he'd go see who the mysterious visitor was, and what he wanted, since the old guy wasn't going to say. As he walked by, Nolen's grin grew. Now Luke knew something was definitely up. Something big. Nolen's smiles were as rare as two-dollar bills.

Luke enjoyed his newfound freedom as he walked down the short hall to the foyer. He'd forced himself to give up his cane almost a week ago. Moving with care, he'd regained his equilibrium and added a bit of speed to his gait. Avery had been complimentary of his progress, though he could see the sadness beneath her smile. One step closer to freedom. One step closer to leaving...her.

Something he hadn't figured out how to handle yet.

Behind him, he could hear multiple sets of footsteps as his brothers and Nolen followed. He hoped whatever stood outside the door wasn't an embarrassment.

As he stepped out the front door onto the veranda, Luke's eyes were drawn to the shiny black hot rod in the drive. The sleek, low-slung coupe set his heart racing the way most men's would for a sexy woman. Behind him, he heard a masculine whistle of appreciation that echoed his own feelings.

Then the driver's-side door opened, and out stepped Avery. Her buttery-soft tan pants and leather jacket finally drew his gaze away from the car. The uncertain edges of her smile tugged at something in his chest he couldn't name. She closed the door and stepped around the car to meet them on the porch.

"What's all this?" he asked, his gesture encompassing the car that she couldn't have gotten anywhere around here.

She glanced at all the men in the small space, then turned all her focus back to him. She probably thought it was a safer option.

"I came to give you the good news," she said. "I've had all your X-rays and evaluation results looked over by your doctor. You passed. It's time to drive again."

Luke stared for a moment, not quite comprehending her words. They'd talked about his driving as being something he would do *in the future*, but she'd never given him a firm date. He'd known she was evaluating his progress this week, but didn't question why. He'd known he was on the right track. He'd just hoped to learn how far along it he was.

Now he knew.

The smile that burst over his face had originated deep in his gut. Pats on his back from his brothers only added to the joy.

"Very good, Master Luke," Nolen said.

But it was the beaming face before him that held his attention. Her joy reflected his. He couldn't stop himself. He drew her close and met her lips with his own, felt the spark of that touch.

By the time he pulled away, she was flushed and panting. His brothers were grinning. "You're welcome," she murmured.

She waved her hand in the car's direction. "I thought we could celebrate. And I didn't think you wanted to have your first drive in my little SUV."

"You didn't rent this car anywhere around here," Jacob remarked, echoing Luke's earlier thoughts.

Avery shrugged. "The Blackstones aren't the only people who know people."

The men gave a murmur of appreciation that had Avery's cheeks flushing even deeper. She reached in a pocket of those skintight pants and pulled out the keys with a metallic rattle. Then she held them out. "Shall we go?"

Luke grabbed her hand and started down the steps, wishing he could sprint. "See y'all later."

He was able to stay his excitement long enough to open her door, then he practically ran to the other side of the car. But after dropping into the low leather seat, Luke found himself unable to move. Beside him, Avery kept quiet.

The seat felt cool, smooth. As he squeezed his hands around the steering wheel, the familiar feel overwhelmed him. His chest tightened. One hand dropped to the stick shift in the center console. He'd learned to drive on a stick and all his personal cars had been manual transmission ever since. His memories reverberated with the hum of the engine beneath his body, the pressure of the pedals beneath his feet and the shift of the stick beneath his palm. The scent of leather filled his senses, along with the sweet scent of woman.

Avery.

Blinking his eyes, Luke cleared his vision, then turned to her. She blinked back, sitting still with her hands folded in her lap. "Sorry," he said, then realized he didn't need to apologize. Understanding shone from her blue eyes, accompanied by a sweet little smile.

"Let's go," she said.

He pushed the ignition button. A smooth purr filled the small cabin and Luke's entire body went *ahhh*...

Then he revved the engine and shifted into gear. Control was the only option. Luke kept himself to a snail's pace as they started down the drive. The ache to pick up speed sat heavy in his gut, but he knew the minute he gave in, his small exertion of will would break and he'd never get it back.

He carefully gauged every turn, every acceleration. They headed out on the highway, opposite the direction of town. The first time he hit sixty should have felt like nothing compared to his racing stints, but instead his heart pounded same as the first time he'd put tires to a track.

He was ultra-aware of his precious cargo. Avery—

who'd gone out of her way to do this. Who'd given him this gift.

Acute awareness of how undermined his confidence had been by the accident shook him. The fact that he wouldn't let himself gun it. Couldn't. Because something bad might happen. And Avery sat next to him in the car.

Just when the shaking reached his hands, a warm palm covered the upper part of his forearm. He eased off the gas and looked over at Avery.

"Turn right up here," she said.

Reorienting himself to his surroundings, he realized they were about ten miles out from Blackstone Manor. The road, and the turnoff, should have been familiar to him. His late teens had practically been lived on this road.

He followed her directions down the road to the entrance beyond. "I didn't realize this place was still here," he said.

"I got the owner to open it up for you. He's kept it in good repair, but they only race here once a month now." She chuckled. "He remembers you very well, and appreciated the memorabilia you sent him a couple of years ago."

Wow. Avery had arranged for him to spend his first time back behind the wheel since his accident at the only racetrack within fifty miles. Probably more like seventy-five. "Do you trust me to do this?"

"I'm trusting you to know your abilities...and your limits."

Would he push it too hard? He knew firsthand how addictive speed was, how desperately the fever burned in his blood for it. But as he looked into her direct gaze, her words echoed inside him.

A few minutes later, he halted the car on the lane. To his surprise, Avery unbuckled her seat belt.

"That's not safe, hon," he said.

"It's not a problem if I'm not gonna be in the car."

He sucked in his breath, simply watching her.

Her soft hand rubbed along his jawline. "I know you'd never tell me, but I have a feeling this is something you need to do by yourself. Right?"

Not by nod nor shake did he give away his answer, but she got out anyway. Waiting until she was safely behind the barricade, he eased the car into gear and took a very slow turn around the track. It had been years since he'd been on an oval track this small. He let himself and the car meld with the road. Then he took a deep breath, down into the bottom of his lungs, and hit the gas.

Forty minutes later, he wanted to cry true tears at having to stop, but knew he shouldn't press the limit of his healing limbs…or his therapist. But as he drove off the track, he knew this would stand out as one of the most important moments of his life.

Not just his career.

Twelve

As Luke hit the straightaway leading from town to Blackstone Manor, he couldn't help but sadly remember the black sports coupe Avery had rented for him. It made him miss his race car, and the beaut he normally drove every day. Instead he was driving a pickup from the Blackstone fleet.

His foot pressed harder on the gas, giving him the thrill of speed and the satisfaction of being that much closer to Avery. His woman.

After a long day walking the mill for inspections, he wanted only one type of thrill tonight—one that involved bare skin and delicious friction and hard thrusts.

It sure beat watching the door at the mill to see if Mark was going to walk through. Word must have gotten out that Luke would be there today, because the ladies in the office had said Mark decided to take personal time at the last minute. That guy had better hide. If Luke ever heard him talk to Avery, or any woman, like that again, his job wouldn't be the only thing Mark would have to worry about losing.

Maybe that straight, pretty-boy nose of his…

Luke gunned it a little harder, speeding down the road to get to the Manor, get his clothes, talk to Jacob about today and then get himself over to Avery's. Thoughts of Avery's house distracted him from his impatience. It was weird. He'd never felt at home at Blackstone Manor, or his apartment, or anywhere else. But he loved Avery's home.

Slightly smaller than the Manor, it only had three stories. She'd closed off the upper floor completely. But the light atmosphere, complemented by lots of blond wood and soothing colors, made his whole body relax. He shouldn't enjoy being there that much. Shouldn't daydream about what it would be like to live there every day, to play with Avery in the woods and eat dinner with her in the breakfast nook. To sleep beside her every night listening to the serenade of frogs and crickets outside.

He. Should. Not. Go. There.

So why did he?

Before he could answer that—or avoid answering it—he heard a pop from under the hood. He barely had time to frown before the truck pulled sharply to the left. There wasn't time to think, only react. When all was said and done, he was facing the opposite direction, hanging at a forty-five-degree angle off the side of the road. A side glance confirmed a deep water drainage ditch dug out between the road and the fields waited below him. Even worse, anything not concrete or asphalt had turned into a muddy mess after three solid days of steady rain. He could feel the incremental slips of the heavy vehicle as the top layer of soil started to give way.

Not the most stable of positions, but luckily Luke had done extensive upper body work. He was able to lift himself through the open window rather than shifting the balance by opening the door. Once he had his feet back on the asphalt, he watched the steady slide of the truck the rest of the way down the hill into about five feet of water with a bit more detachment than before. For a moment, anyway.

But then the memories rushed over him. As if his body equated this incident with the last car accident— the one he didn't walk away from—his knees went weak. Thankful there was no one to see, he let himself go down. Silence reverberated around him. His mind replayed the sounds of screaming metal, the smell of gasoline and the burning sting of smoke. But above all came the pain, like his lower body was being torn to shreds. Every laceration had been on fire, though emergency personnel had reached him before the car could erupt into actual flames.

Once the shaking stopped and the nausea subsided, Luke pulled his cell phone from the case attached to his belt. A simple call to Jacob. A few deep breaths to get himself back on his feet. He took a mental inventory of all his limbs, not finding any major issues. Some tightening in his lower back. Oh, and upper back. Hell, he was tight all over.

Great. No hiding that from Avery.

A sound in the distance had him looking in the direction of the Manor. He could see Jacob's Tahoe as it came around the bend and sped toward him. Another dark vehicle followed behind.

Only the sound of engines came in stereo. Looking in the other direction, Luke could see flashing lights and cursed. He should have kept his suspicions that this hadn't been an accident to himself. Jacob had taken the initiative and called the authorities. So now Luke would spend the night answering questions and filling out paperwork. Lovely.

Jacob pulled over to the side of the road and parked. He stopped about five feet away, arms crossed over his chest as he studied the truck. "Well, good thing you know what you're doin'."

"I agree."

A glance down the highway at the oncoming vehicles had Jacob stepping forward quickly. A single strong hug had Luke's back muscles wincing, but he wasn't gonna complain. He could feel Jacob's relief that he was okay without his twin even having to say it.

A low whistle from behind his brother separated them. Luke glanced over Jacob's shoulder to Zachary Gatlin, who must have been in the black SUV.

"Man, that takes some mad skills. How'd you manage not to roll it?" Zach asked.

Luke rubbed at the back of his neck. "Honestly, I'm not sure. All I remember is the noise, then it's a blur."

Zach nodded. "Instincts took over. Great job."

It didn't feel like a great job. It felt like a flashback from a hell he'd hoped never to endure again. He simply nodded and left it at that.

Luke had never been happier that Aiden had hired

Zach. The new head of their personal security handled most of the police issues, except for the questioning. He had the truck towed and kept everyone on task. Luke only protested when an ambulance showed up and Jacob insisted Luke let them look him over.

"The only thing wrong with me is some tight muscles."

"You never know," Jacob said.

"I don't need it."

He should have known by the look on his brother's face that resistance was futile. Twenty minutes later, Avery's little SUV joined the immobile caravan parked along one lane of the highway. The rest of the scant traffic headed out this way had been diverted into the other lane. "Oh, man—you didn't."

Jacob just smirked. "You should have listened to me the first time."

Damn married men.

Avery's steps were snappy, but she didn't rush. He could almost see her taking everything in despite the fading light. Especially him. Those astute therapist eyes traveled over every inch of his body. It wasn't the kind of inspection he'd been hoping for, but then again, this evening wasn't turning out the way he'd envisioned at all.

"Are you all right?" she asked, rushing right up to him. For once, she didn't look around at their audience before touching him. Her arms widened as if to hug him, but she settled for grasping his biceps instead. "Do you hurt anywhere?"

Instead of answering, he reached around her, pulling her close. Her warmth seeped into his body, into

his bones. He pressed his lips against the smooth softness of her hair. "I'm great, now that you're here."

Her body relaxed into his, but she didn't completely give in. "But you couldn't call me yourself?"

Thanks, Jacob. "Once we were done here, I was
going to get another truck and head over to your
house."

"Would you have told me?"

No. "I didn't want you to worry."

"Well, I did. We need to get you back to the house,
to check everything out and make sure there was no
damage."

"That's what I told him," Jacob said as he approached.

Luke shot daggers at his brother with his gaze.
"I'm fine. The paramedics said so."

She pulled back, leaving his tired body without
warmth or support. "They don't know what they
should specifically be looking for based on your his-
tory," Avery said. "I'll feel better once I've checked
you out." She looked over at Jacob, then past him to
the police officers wrapping everything up. Every-
where but at Luke. "If you don't mind."

Luke looked at Jacob, unsure of what to do. His
brother shrugged, no help whatsoever.

Right now, Luke knew just what he wanted. He'd
deal with the aftermath of the wreck tomorrow. "Let's
go home."

Avery stepped back even more, wrapping her arms
around her middle.

"Call my cell if you need anything else," Luke said
to Jacob. Then he walked toward Avery's car, using an
arm around her shoulders to turn her to go with him.

* * *

Avery could sense Luke's disappointment when he came out of the bathroom and found her still in her scrubs. Men. She was rapidly learning that the old adage was true. They did constantly think about one thing.

"I thought we were going to bed early," he said hopefully.

She shook her head, secretly amused but keeping her therapist facade firmly in place. "Not yet. But if you cooperate, you might get a reward." She pointed for him to lie on the bed.

Part of her felt shocked. A month ago, she could never have imagined herself teasing about sex. But with Luke, it came naturally. And he teased her back, which made her giggle, but deep inside she stored sadness away. Because one day he would leave, and this magical time would be over.

"I want to check you out—" she started.

"Go right ahead, baby—"

"—for any damage."

His sigh echoed around her spacious bedroom. "I told you, I'm fine. Just a little tight, that's all."

This time her hands went to her hips and her attitude showed up full force. "You want some help with that, right?"

He glanced over his shoulder, his face aglow. "As in, a massage?"

Hook 'em quick. "Yes, as in a massage." She held up a warning hand. "But if you're going to be difficult…"

He settled onto the bed on his belly without another word. She needed to remember what good currency massages were. Stepping to the side of the bed, she started with his feet and worked her way up. Her palms found every knot in his normally smooth muscles, working them out. She savored his groans as much as the feel of his skin.

Only when he'd melted into a metaphorical puddle of goo did she deliver the bad news. "Well, this has set you back a bit, I'm afraid."

He lifted up on his elbows to look at her over his shoulder. "What?"

Her hands found the small areas where she could feel the changes from the last time she'd touched him. "It's minor. Some muscle damage here in your lower legs from braking so hard. Which created a chain reaction up your leg."

Her stomach quivered as she thought about him in that truck, struggling for control. Thank God he had extensive skills, or the wreck would have been devastating, what with those banks on either side of the road.

"About a week's worth of extra therapy should fix it, I think." She tried to lighten her tone. "Are you sure this wasn't a ploy to keep seeing me? A few extra massages, maybe?"

Luke rolled over onto his back, lifting himself into a sitting position against the headboard in one fluid movement. He leaned into the pillows, fully unaware that he'd laid out a smorgasbord of sexiness that she was more than ready to dive into.

"I'm not sure," he said, giving her a look that said he knew exactly where this was leading. "Is that all you have to offer me for sticking around? A few massages?"

How about my heart? But she wouldn't say that, so she countered with "Are you saying my massages aren't good enough? Maybe I'll save them for another deserving patient."

Luke reared up, grabbing her by her upper arms and dragging her down onto the bed with him. Or rather, *on* him. He was the best kind of lumpy mattress—the living, breathing kind.

"Oh no, woman. Those massages are mine." He planted a hard kiss against her lips. "All mine."

"Sounds perfect." She froze for a minute, wondering if she'd gone too far, but he didn't react to her words.

Instead he focused on her body, their bodies. Lifting her up with those glorious biceps, he helped her straddle him. Her knees naturally fell open on each side of his hips, her thin scrubs leaving nothing to the imagination. Luke's boxer briefs molded to his erection like a second skin. The position brought them into perfect alignment, and Avery's core went soft.

She pressed down, lightly grinding against him, savoring the differences between them. Luke groaned as he dug his hands into her hair. He pulled her down, teasing her mouth open. Not that she needed much coaxing. The feel of his tongue inside her mouth, like she wanted him inside her body, liquefied her. She met him stroke for stroke.

Luke's hands fisted at her sides, clenching the material from her top, which pressed her bra into her nipples. She gasped, the sensations building.

Then the world disappeared for a moment as he swept the top up over her head. Moving fast, he unclasped her bra. As cool air rushed over her, she moaned, but heat quickly followed. Luke's large hands shaped her, molded her, engendering a lovely boneless sensation that left her melting. His mouth at her breast swept away the last of her thoughts, until she could only feel.

Her thighs tensed, rubbing her most sensitive spot against him. Building the tension just where she needed it. As if he'd read her mind, Luke's hands went to her waistband and jerked with just the right amount of force. The material parted and her body went wild.

Soon she was completely naked, and riding Luke Blackstone. She didn't even have the sense to be embarrassed.

For once, Avery felt a surge of power rise. This was her show. Her time. She dipped her hips, just an inch, teasing him. He gasped, then groaned when she pulled back up. Over and over she moved, until they both broke out in a sweat.

Only when she thought she'd die without him did she sink down—one long slide until her thighs met his, and she felt stretched almost to her limit. But now Luke wanted the upper hand. His palms cupped her hips, those long fingers pressing against her flesh. His touch guided her, pleasuring them both with a hard rhythm that shook her breath in her chest. She gave herself over to his demands.

Not just her body, but her soul. No barriers. No hesitation. Her hands on his shoulders sought safety, even though there was none to be had. There never would be.

Just as she cried out, Luke stiffened. Her body tightened around his, and she dug her fingers into his skin as she exploded—oblivion quick and almost painful.

Then she lay next to him in the dark, listening to his breath even out. As he slipped into sleep, she ached for what she so desperately wanted.

But would never have.

Thirteen

Luke glanced at Jacob next to him at the bar, waiting for his fiancée to bring them drinks. KC was being helped by her brother, Zach. He wasn't officially working, but he still kept a close, protective eye on his family. Luke couldn't blame him.

"This was a great idea," Luke said, grinning as he watched his reserved older brother, Aiden, lead his wife onto the dance floor—for a fast song, no less.

He usually pictured Aiden drinking imported beer and fine dining in New York, not dancing in a honky-tonk in South Carolina. Boy, had times changed.

Jacob grinned as KC approached. "We all needed some downtime. The past few days have been intense."

"Definitely," Luke replied.

With all the suspicions and questions running

through Luke's mind, he'd been hard-pressed to think about anything else. Except Avery. She consumed him on so many levels now.

Their mission for adventures had gotten derailed by his accident, then their utter physical absorption of each other. They'd spent every night wrapped up in the big bed, shutting out the world.

Luke was more than addicted…each time he visited, he was in danger of never leaving her house again.

But tonight, he wouldn't be sidetracked. If he couldn't have Avery in bed, he wanted her on the dance floor. Another adventure. After all, he couldn't recall ever seeing her dance.

He positioned her next to him on a small bit of dance floor real estate and glanced around to see what everyone else was doing. After two minutes, he had no idea why Avery didn't normally dance—she was deadly at it. She picked up the steps quickly and executed them with incredibly sexy hip action that had his mouth watering.

Luke, on the other hand, knew that he danced with more enthusiasm than skill. When he missed a step, they both laughed and kept going.

He hadn't laughed that much in a long time.

After a handful of songs, he led her back to the table for some cool drinks and bar food. Avery eyed him over her French fry.

"What?"

"You seem quite fond of surprises," she said, grinning despite her accusing tone.

"Worked, didn't it?"

Her grin turned rueful. "Guess so."

"No guessing about it." He leaned closer, invading her space until he saw the brown flecks in her eyes. "No sexy woman should be left sitting on the sidelines. You have too much to offer for that."

He watched the flush build in her cheeks. Her eyes widened, then sparkled with a look he now knew all too well. Leaning in, he brushed her lips with his, aching for more than he could have right now.

As he pulled back, he was glad to see she didn't look around, didn't peek to see who was watching. Her entire focus was trained on him...and his on her.

"Sometimes sitting on the sidelines becomes a habit, because it's familiar," she said quietly. "It's comfortable. And we know it won't end up hurting us."

"Won't it? In the long run?"

Excuses were just that. Experience had taught him he got nowhere when he let those little half-truths direct his actions. He wanted to pull her against him and tell her it would be okay, that neither of them would hurt when this was over. But he couldn't. That was a guarantee he didn't think he'd be able to live up to. A buzz in his pocket saved him from answering.

Pulling out his cell phone, Luke saw his crew chief's number on the screen. With a gesture to Avery, he hurried for the door.

When he'd stepped into the cool night air, free from the music of the noisy bar, he answered.

"Hey, Jeff. What's up?"

They'd had regular check-ins, but Jeff hated the phone so he never called just to chat.

"Got some great news, buddy."

Anticipation added to the buzz he'd worked up

from dancing. Luke walked across the parking lot to burn off his sudden burst of adrenaline. "Hit me."

"Our sponsor problem is solved."

"How come?" Luke tried to ignore the pounding of his heart in his throat.

"I was contacted tonight by someone whose interest is off the scales. You're not gonna believe this."

Probably not. "Who?"

"NC State Oil."

Hot damn. One of the biggest sponsors in his division. Luke's knees went a little weak.

"Bobby Joe is retiring," Jeff said. "Very down low right now. They want you as their new feature car."

Jeff rattled off some other details but Luke wasn't processing them. Only when the words "come back" rang in his ear did he return to earth.

"When?" he asked, his mouth dry as cotton.

"Next season, buddy. They're all set to negotiate, talk contracts."

Luke thought over Avery's careful plans, her goal of getting him back to racing—in two seasons.

Jeff was oblivious. "I'll give the head honcho your number. You can set up a meeting."

Luke barely remembered signing off. He couldn't move, standing alone in the cool night air.

A second chance.

All that he'd wanted since his accident was to return to the track, to his career. Now he could. So why wasn't he screwing up his recovery by jumping for joy?

Deep down, he knew why. Because there was more than just her disappointment keeping him from returning to the bar and breaking the news to Avery.

The pain on the horizon wasn't only physical…and wasn't only his.

Almost to the building, the sound of an angry voice halted Luke's stride.

"I said I'd get you your money. I just need more time."

Luke instinctively stepped into the shadows, not far from where Mark Zabinski was speaking into his cell phone. His agitated tone indicated intense strain.

"Look—I realize I've gotten a little behind—"

His heavy sigh permeated the gloom.

"—okay, a lot. But I'll take care of it."

Another silence. Luke strained to hear beyond the pounding of his heart, surprised when Mark's voice turned whiny. "No, I can't just go to my parents for any more handouts. I told you, I can fix this." He exhaled a ragged breath.

"Forty-eight hours. Got it."

As Luke slipped back through the door into the club, he couldn't help wondering what that had been all about.

Life was too damn complicated.

Luke looked around Zach's garage at the men who'd supported him after his accident, and couldn't find the words to tell them someone had tried to kill him. Even though the evidence sat right before him, the words were hard to come by.

Luckily Zach started the conversation for him. "So do you have an idea about who's trying to hurt you yet, or do we need to do some digging?"

The shock spread in low murmurs. Luke had to face the truth he'd been avoiding. "I'm pretty sure I know who it is. I've only had problems with one person since my return."

Zach patted the truck's hood. "A certain someone who thinks you're stealing his girl?"

They all looked at Zach in surprise. Not because Zach was saying something Luke hadn't thought, but because he hadn't realized anyone else knew.

Zach smirked. "I snooped around once they towed the truck in. It's definitely been tampered with."

"Dammit." Jacob's gaze darted between Luke and the vehicle. "How long have you known this?"

"I knew the truck had been messed with right away," Luke said. He shook his head. "Mark and I had a few run-ins over Avery, but I never thought he was that vindictive." Until Mark came to Avery's house— that had been eye-opening. "Actually, I think I started suspecting him of something from the moment I stepped into the executive suite. He made me uneasy, but there was no reason to think it was anything more than that."

But there was more. "While I was outside the bar last night, I overheard a conversation between Mark and someone who wanted money from him. Badly."

Aiden asked the obvious. "What does that have to do with us congregating in Zach's garage?"

"It got me thinking." Luke paced a few steps. "The way he talked, it was obvious that he needed to raise cash, quickly. Whoever was on the other end of the line was more than unhappy. And it didn't sound like the first time."

He looked at Jacob. "One of the departments he oversees is accounting, right? He's fought to keep an outdated computer system. How many people check those paper files?"

Jacob was catching on. "That antiquated system would be the perfect tool for embezzling money," he mused. "Do you really think he'd do this? I mean, his family has money."

"Were you friends with him in high school?" Zach asked.

"We call it that now," Jacob answered, "but truthfully, we were rivals. Healthy competition for a lot of the same roles kept us motivated."

Zach glanced at Luke, who shrugged. "I had no motivation." And no guilt over never serving on student council.

Jacob threw out his former taunt. "Slacker."

"That's me," Luke said with a grin. "I just drive round and round in a circle for a living."

"It's a good thing you do," Zach said. "Otherwise, your ass would be grass. This probably wouldn't even have been too big a problem for you, except you were on a road flanked by steep ditches."

"Too bad you headed home instead of to Avery's," Jacob added.

"Nope. Probably for the best," Luke contradicted. "I drive over two narrow bridges to get to her place."

Zach winced. "Yeah, that would have been worse."

"But do we know for sure it's really sabotage?" Aiden asked.

Zach took them on a tour of Luke's truck, showing them the difference between wear and deliberate damage.

Jacob looked puzzled. "Does he really hate you enough to seriously harm you?"

"I wouldn't have thought so." Luke glanced back under the hood, remembering his last conversation with Mark. "But I did threaten his job the last time I saw him." He briefly explained what had happened.

Aiden's expression darkened. "You were fully in the right. Avery didn't deserve that."

Zachary cleared his throat. "I hate to bring this up, but it's part of my job to be suspicious." He met gazes with each man in turn. "Based on everything we've talked about here, is anyone else worried about the mischief a high-ranking employee with unlimited access to financial accounts and a possible gambling problem can get into roaming around the mill?"

Luke stiffened as a lightbulb lit up in his brain. He could see the moment it happened to Jacob and Aiden, too. So he asked for all of them, "You think he might be involved with the sabotage of the mill, too?"

Zach held up his hands. "I'm saying he might have motive for more than just vehicle tampering."

"But if the mill goes under, he'd lose his job, and the money," Luke pointed out.

"Not if he has a new source of income from a rival mill," Zach said. "They could pay him to do it, then offer him a higher position in their company once the competition is shut down."

A chorus of male curses filled the garage.

After a minute Zach said, "We don't know for sure. We need a way to find out."

"At least there's one easy place to look," Jacob said. "His accounts at the office are our best chance of finding hard evidence of embezzlement…or anything else." He shifted, obviously upset with the idea. "If it's not on the system, we're out of luck."

"Guess I'll volunteer to do some snooping," Luke said. "I'll go at night so few people will be around, but if they see me, I can just claim to be going over the accounts to acquaint myself with the business."

But first he owed Avery a long-overdue confession.

Fourteen

"It's okay, Cindy. I'll close up when I'm done."

Her office manager sent Avery a tired wave. After the long day they'd put in, she didn't have to be told to leave twice. Today had been one of those days where everything that could go wrong, had. From surly patients to computer errors to missing records, it had all hit the fan today.

Avery wished more than anything she could just close her eyes and drift away for a while. Maybe she'd enjoy the facility's whirlpool before going home. Her muscles throbbed their approval of the idea.

They ached from wanting other things, too. She'd been asleep this morning when Luke had headed out. He'd left a note that he'd see her tonight, but she'd heard nothing since.

Right now, she just wanted to relax. With the front

doors locked, she shut everything else down. Grateful that she kept some clothes here, she started the tub with the water as hot as she could stand. Normally she would have put in bath salts, but she just wanted the jets tonight.

She'd just stripped down when her phone dinged. Glancing at it, she saw a text from Luke.

At the door. Brought dinner. Hungry?

She couldn't resist. Only Luke ever tempted her to be sexy, fun Avery.

In more ways than one. Hope you brought an appetite.

She grabbed an oversize towel and headed through the dark building to the front doors. She turned the key in the lock, then opened the door for Luke. He must not have noticed her state of undress until he was completely in, because he stopped abruptly. "Avery?"

Without missing a beat, she relocked the door, then headed back the way she'd come. First she let the towel droop, revealing her bare back, almost to the dimples right above her butt. After another few yards, and she let the towel fall completely, trailing behind her from the corner still clutched in her hand. She heard Luke's footsteps behind her, his sharp intake of breath, and knew he could see her pale skin in the gloom.

By the time he'd set down the food, she'd stepped into the swirling hot water of the tub. Kneeling, she let the water engulf her to the small of her back, then glanced over her shoulder at Luke. The way his gaze clung to her dampening skin was gratifying. Flattering. Desire clutched low in her body.

She heard the soft slip of clothes against skin as he undressed. Then the hiss of his breath as he stepped into the steamy water. Bubbles attacked her skin from all sides. Anticipation heated her up. Need clawed at her, forcing her to glance at him once more, the invitation clear.

He crowded in close. The heat from him and the water shot her to supernova status. His hardness tucked against her, fitting snugly into the crease of her backside. She pressed into him.

How could he make her feel so good? A simple touch, a look, and her confidence soared. Or maybe it was just her desires overwhelming her self-consciousness. It just felt good to feel free. To not be afraid of doing something stupid.

His heavy palms against her breasts left her reeling. Her nipples tightened, needing his touch. He played with them, sending sensation shooting through her. How would she ever live without his touch?

He knew just when to tease, just when to move. His whole body rolled against hers, skin to slick skin. As if no part of him could hold back.

Her body grew hypersensitive, feeling every droplet of sweat as it beaded, every tremble of her breasts and every forceful stroke of him inside her. His thrusts shortened, his groans dragging from his lungs as he drove them both higher. Finally on the brink, she felt his mouth cover the sensitive spot where her neck met her shoulder. He sucked hard, as if to devour every ounce of her he could reach.

One final drive and they exploded together. Their cries mingled in the steamy mist coating the room. Bodies milked every last twitch of sensation before collapsing into the water. Sated. Satisfied.

If she weren't in a tub, Avery knew she'd slip right under the veil into sleep. In just a few minutes she'd get up and dry and dress. Just not yet. Not yet. But Luke was having none of it. All too soon, she was on her feet on the chilly tile floor.

As he rubbed her with a towel, she barely heard Luke's voice above the sound of the draining water. Not enough to distinguish what he was saying. "What?" she asked, struggling to open her heavy eyelids.

Her first peek told her something was wrong. For the first time ever, she'd guess that Luke Blackstone was…nervous. This time when he spoke she heard him more clearly. "I've got a new race car sponsor."

Did he say… She twisted to see his face as he moved to her back. "A sponsor? So soon?"

"Yeah. Pretty amazing, huh?" A slight grin pulled at his lips. But what worried her was his hooded look. "And it's a good one, too. A great one."

"That's wonderful." Wasn't it?

"The company is one of the biggest sponsors on the circuit right now," he said, but he still wouldn't look at her. "Their current driver is about to retire, and they want me to take his place."

"So they're willing to wait until you're fully recovered?"

His lack of words and lack of expression didn't

bode well. If she hadn't been this close to him, she wouldn't have noticed the rapid beat of his pulse at the base of his throat. Nerves? Or simply the aftermath of what they'd just done together?

Avery, herself, was quickly cooling down—in a very uncomfortable way.

"Actually," he finally said, clearly and unnaturally calmly, "they want me back for next season."

"And you told them they had to wait, right?" Avery wasn't even sure why she asked. She knew from Luke's previous remarks she was fighting a losing battle.

"No. I didn't."

Without warning, he snagged a towel from the counter and wrapped it around himself, almost as if girding for battle, leaving her open, vulnerable.

Needing something to do, anything that didn't involve waiting for him to return to her, she set the tub to drain. Though he wasn't looking in her direction, her self-consciousness had already returned full force. She too rushed for a towel, stumbling a bit as she moved.

Luckily, she regained her feet and got herself covered without incident. Landing flat on her face, naked, would have been the ultimate humiliation—especially when she needed him to listen to her. She hadn't managed to get through to him before. Would she be able to now?

"Luke, that's really not what's best for you, for your body. It takes time for these things to not only heal, but for you to regain strength."

"I'm already getting around fine. No cane." He whipped around to face her. How could a man look so intimidating with only a towel on, his long blond hair sexily disheveled? "I'm back on my feet when they thought I might never be. If I continue strength training, I'll be just fine."

"Will you? I explained what happened after the accident the other night. The stress that type of incident puts on your body can be tremendous. The risks when it's happening on the track are so high. Please don't—" She choked herself off.

Begging him to stay here, not to go, would have nothing to do with risks and everything to do with herself. But personal desires couldn't have anything to do with her argument right now.

He braced his legs, as if taking a stand. Against her.

"Am I well enough to go back out on the track?"

Oh, she didn't want to do this. "Yes, but if something happens—"

"I'm well enough to do my job. That's what matters."

Stubborn man. "But a wreck on the track could do irreparable damage because you haven't built up enough resistance. You know all too well how dangerous your job can be."

His cold stare told her she'd crossed a line. "Is that really your argument or is this about something else?"

Avery jerked back as if he'd slapped her. "What?"

"Are you sure this isn't about you and me? Is it that you want me to stay, and this is the only argument you can think of to keep me here?"

Oh, she'd thought his insinuation had hurt. This was a whole other level. She fell back on her professional persona, simply dropping the towel and pulling her scrubs back over her damp, naked body. Only when she was covered and her hair was smoothed back did she ask, "Are you seriously questioning whether I'm letting my personal feelings sway my judgment?" If it was one thing she'd always prided herself on, it was that her evaluation of Luke had been first and foremost professional. Always. She could feel her own anger rise. "Would you rather I just tell you to stop being a stubborn jackass and listen to reason?"

"That's exactly what I'm asking. I mean, you've been waiting for this for an awfully long time. Maybe you can't bear to see it end. Will there be another excuse coming down the line after this one?"

"I don't want you to go." She swallowed. Keeping her emotions under control was so much harder than she'd imagined. "I'll be the first to acknowledge I've developed feelings for you...deep feelings. But I've always known you would leave, Luke. Always." Which was why she'd never verbalized those feelings.

He stood there like a mountain, arms crossed over that magnificent chest. Not giving an inch.

"But my professional opinion is just that—professional. My recommendations were backed up by your former physical therapist and your physician before we ever became involved. I would never mix that in with my—" she took a deep breath "—personal feelings for you."

She let the words hang in the air, hoping he would at least acknowledge the truth of what she was saying, but he didn't.

And that was something she couldn't live with.

"If you truly think my evaluation of you, my recommendation for your career, is based on a selfish need to keep me with you, some obsessive desire to fulfill a childhood crush—" man, was that humiliating "—then I think it's time you left."

Without waiting for his nonresponse, she swept by and stalked to her office, locking herself inside before she collapsed against the door. Silent tears trickled down her cheeks. Only after she heard him open the front doors and leave did she give in to the storm inside her.

She'd be strong later. She'd clean the tub, lock the doors and return to her empty house, just like she had every night before Luke had come back into her life. Later.

For now, she could only let the pain sweep her away from the knowledge that once again, someone would leave her behind.

Man, I am such a jackass.

Luke had always prided himself on being kind and friendly. He rarely had conflict with anyone. When he did, he'd just as soon avoid it by disappearing onto the track than provoking major fights like his brother Aiden sometimes did. Luke was a fan of letting things work themselves out.

Sure, he occasionally said things that rubbed people the wrong way. Not out of any desire to be mean, just from letting something slip that would have been better left unsaid. Just like a few nights ago with Avery. He'd known the minute he'd started talking about feelings he was gonna screw up. And sure enough, he'd dug a hole so deep he'd been stumped as to how to get himself out of it.

Now he had to figure out how to salvage the one thing that had touched him like nothing but his racing ever had. But should he? Was it fair to win her back, patch things up, then turn around and leave her behind so he could pursue his dream?

He didn't know. Pacing back and forth in his suite at Blackstone Manor had only made his leg ache, reminding him of Avery all the more. He couldn't stop thinking about his truck, either. There were too many reasons to suspect Mark had tampered with it, regardless of whether his intentions were deadly or not. Then Zach had texted him:

Found multiple log-ins from Mark's work computer to the inventory system. Only accessible by management. Possible link to sabotage.

So instead of sleeping, wrapped around Avery's warm, silky body tonight, he was poking through Mark's computer at the mill. What else was he going to do at two o'clock in the morning?

Not to mention, he had no idea if the guy might strike again. And Luke wasn't losing his life over some agenda he didn't even understand. Tonight was the best night, because the plant was shut down for maintenance that would begin in the morning.

It didn't take long. After an hour of snooping, Luke had enough evidence to confirm some of his suspicions…and awaken even more. Mark didn't know nearly enough about computers to hide what he'd been doing, or maybe he'd thought he didn't need to. The combination of a dated system and paper files had allowed him to move money without anyone noticing. The withdrawals from various company funds into a secondary account that Mark then transferred to a miscellaneous account at another bank appeared genuine enough, until someone searched for the documentation and receipts.

The deposits had grown in frequency and amount over the past few years. Since his work performance had been fine, Luke didn't think it was drugs or drinking. Gambling was still his best guess.

If Mark was unstable or desperate, he could hurt a lot of people by sabotaging the mill, even if he simply intended to destroy property. Just like the goons he'd probably hired had done to Aiden's studio.

Luke copied what he could into his online backup storage before shutting the system down. Rubbing his eyes, he blinked at the clock. Three-thirty in the morning. Maybe now he could sleep without aching for Avery by his side, her measured breath a soothing rhythm beneath the palm of his hand. First thing tomorrow, he'd meet with Jacob, Aiden and Zach.

Firing this guy outright wasn't the solution. They had to be very careful to get all the information they needed before confronting Mark.

Closing down the office, he headed for the stairwell. The accounting department was on the third floor, so Luke decided to exit via the stairs. After sitting so long, moving felt good. As he passed the door for level two, he heard a truck engine rev.

Knowing there wasn't supposed to be any activity tonight, Luke paused. The administrative offices sat over a two-story loading dock, where they shipped out the finished products.

Were they prepping some last-minute deliveries?

That didn't make sense, because the whole plant closed down over maintenance weekend. Maybe it was just his heightened suspicions after everything he'd read tonight, but Luke knew he wouldn't sleep unless he checked it out.

Opening the second-floor entry, he winced as a squeal assaulted the eardrums. The sound echoed through the stairwell. He glanced toward the loading dock below. He couldn't see clearly through the iron mesh of the walkway, but there was definitely a truck. Not one of theirs, though.

He'd have to get closer.

Glancing around, Luke found a wedge to prop the door open. He scooted it closer with his foot, then forced it into place. He could always come back and close it later if this was nothing, but his niggling senses said something was up.

He took the last of the stairs to the ground floor. A turn to the left led down a long hallway to the security entrance. He could jog down there and see if anyone was home, but if no one was, he'd have wasted precious time and legwork. Right would take him down a short distance to the loading dock floor. Better to just take a cautious peek.

Thankfully the lower-level door had been oiled. He eased through with very little noise and stepped out beneath the elevated walkway. He had to lean out for a good look, because of pallets blocking his view. But then he saw the back end of a work van very clearly.

Click.

Luke froze. Anyone from the South recognized that noise—the clear sound of a gun hammer being cocked. He glanced over his shoulder to see Mark watching him with a cool gaze and pointing a pistol directly at him. And if Luke remembered correctly, Mark had taken marksmanship with Jacob in high school. They'd captained rival teams.

"Well, I didn't expect anyone to be here this late, but the fact that it's you is a nice bonus," Mark said.

The snide tone grated across Luke's senses. He turned completely as Mark stepped out of the dappled shadows beneath the walkway.

"Mark, what's going on?" he asked, attempting to keep both his voice and his body loose, casual.

"You showed up just in time," Mark said, his grin stretching a little too far.

"For what? A hunting party?"

Apparently Mark didn't find him funny. "No, you lazy bum. It'll be a celebration, but I doubt you and your intrusive family will see it the same way I do."

"How's that?"

"A giant fireball to celebrate the ruination of the Blackstone brothers and their legacy in Black Hills."

Luke's blood ran cold. Did Mark mean to blow something up? "So you'll destroy the mill in an effort to, what? Get back at me for something?"

Mark jumped forward, the threat of the gun forcing Luke to retreat. "Not 'something,' you ignorant ass. I've spent years working a menial job, always blocked from moving up. I finally got the chance to take my rightful place in management, and you and your brothers decide it's time to ride back into town and save the day." The disgust on his face was perfectly plain. "This place should have been mine. Mine."

Luke's stomach sank. Even though he'd known

Mark needed money, he'd still held on to the idea that his anger at Luke himself centered around Avery. This went far deeper than either of those issues.

He gestured for Luke to turn around. A sharp poke in the back from the gun got him moving forward. Luke tried to keep his steps slow, exaggerating his slight limp. He needed time to figure this out and find a way to get clear.

"I'm not a murderer," Mark said. "Normally I'd say that's taking things a bit too far, you know?" He herded Luke closer to the truck. "But for you, I'll make an exception."

"What makes me so special?"

He jabbed Luke hard in the back, a reward for his smart mouth. "I almost had her where I wanted her, was ready to put a ring on her finger. Then I'd have had all of Avery's money at my disposal and she'd have been none the wiser."

Luke snorted. "Avery Prescott? Are you serious?"

"What the hell's that supposed to mean?"

Luke glanced over his shoulder, just as much to see what Mark was up to as to emphasize his point. "Avery is way too smart to just hand her money over to someone because she married him. She's a good businesswoman. She'd find out about the gambling way before the wedding day."

Luke wasn't sure if the silence that greeted his statement was good or bad. He decided to push his luck.

"Thought you'd kept that pretty secret, didn't you? Why do you think I'm here tonight, Mark?" Luke's disgust hardened his voice. Maybe if he could get Mark riled up, push him off-kilter, he could get the upper hand. "I've been upstairs, going through your computer. All your files. All your emails. I know what you did."

Mark's flush deepened from red to purple. "Doesn't matter. In about fifteen minutes, I'll be the only one who knows. And all that evidence, including you, will have gone up in smoke."

Or so Mark thought. He actually thought Luke wasn't smart enough to have made copies. But Luke *was* smart enough to let him keep believing that... for now.

"And don't bother calling for help. The great advantage of doing this on maintenance weekend is the only people here are the outer guards." Mark laughed. "The local cops haven't figured me out yet and they aren't going to, either."

Maybe Luke could still do something if he could get to a radio and reach a guard, depended on how soon the bomb was set to blow. Fifteen minutes. Luke's adrenaline kicked in hard enough to summon a wave of nausea. This was not gonna be fun.

Without turning his head, he tried to look around, figure out his options. Mark didn't give him enough time. Reaching out for something nearby, he then held it up for Luke to see.

Zip ties.

"Now back up to the door. Nice and slow."

Luke moved himself up to the rear of the van. The whole time, he pumped his fists, hoping to create space once Mark tied him down. As he grabbed at Luke's hands, Luke lifted his wrists slightly against the bar, hoping Mark wouldn't notice.

Luke waited until Mark stepped away with a

smirk. Then he disappeared around the front of the van. Luke heard a door open and some noise. The smell of fertilizer grew. Luke couldn't help but wonder about the size of the bomb.

Mark spoke from inside. "Amazing what you can learn to do on the internet, isn't it? Looks like I'm just making a little delivery for my parents' gardening company and oops—I had an accident."

"Why not just ask them for money?" Luke asked, curious about that since hearing Mark's side of the conversation the other night.

"You know, my older brother reminds me a lot of Jacob. He's soft. Protective. Like my parents don't have more than enough wealth to share. Like I don't deserve it—I'm the one stuck here with them, after all. But not for long. I've found someone else who will pay me very well."

Luke let him ramble while trying to work his hands free. Heaven help him, he would not leave his family, Avery, like this.

"Hasn't done you a lot of good so far, has it?" Luke prodded.

"This one last job and I'll hit the mother lode of payoffs—with a new job to boot. Now shut up and let me work."

While Mark was busy, Luke let his arms straighten once more. Then he squeezed his hands through the extra space he'd created in the ties. Not as much space as he'd like, but luckily he'd started to sweat from nerves and heat. Five minutes and he'd managed to wring his big hands back out.

Luke looked for a weapon, but footsteps told him

he'd run out of time. Mark stepped around the corner. "Time to leave—"

"Yep." Luke swung the heavy half door of the van in Mark's direction, catching his face with a weighty *thunk*.

He didn't stop to check the bomb—he simply grabbed the gun and ran. Adrenaline kept his body from resisting, though Luke had a vague thought he'd be hurting tomorrow.

If there was one.

He reached the door to the hallway, only to find Mark had locked or jammed it somehow. He had to detour to the next door down the line. Damn—why was this room so long? Through that one and back down the hall. This one wasn't a straight shot, so Luke had to guess which turns to take.

He'd maneuvered his way back to the main hall before he heard a voice behind him. "Where are you going, Luke? You'll never make it out in time."

Luke wasn't giving up, but a sudden hard rumble erupted from the middle of the building and Luke knew his time was up. He wasn't going to reach a radio or phone or even a door. He saw the entrance to a room and threw himself into the doorway just as the building seemed to explode around him.

Fifteen

Avery stood in the hallway just outside the emergency room, though she wasn't quite sure how. She didn't remember driving, didn't remember coming inside. Heck, she didn't remember much past Jacob's quick explanation that Luke had been in an explosion at the plant and was being med-flighted to a hospital over an hour away.

She remembered a few choice words from a special newsbreak on the radio—namely *bomb* and *explosion* and *serious injuries*—before she'd turned it off. Not knowing was better than letting vague info whip her into sheer panic.

Common sense told her she shouldn't even be here. After the way Luke had spoken to her the last time they'd been together, it was clear he didn't have a very high opinion of her. Unfortunately, that didn't mute the love that had grown in her heart. Her need to know he was okay overrode all the arguments to stay away that her brain could come up with.

So here she stood. She hadn't been allowed behind the big metal doors to where the family had already gone. After all, she wasn't family, just the woman Luke had been sleeping with for a few weeks. She didn't know if anyone knew she was here. Christina wasn't answering her phone. But she'd wait as long as she had to, until someone came through those doors who could give her news.

It took another forty-five minutes before a familiar face appeared. Christina paused at the nurse's station before looking in her direction. Then she rushed over. Her arms around Avery were the first warmth Avery had felt since she'd received that phone call.

"I'm so sorry," Christina said. "We were speaking with the doctor then Luke woke up and I just didn't think about them not letting you come back to the family waiting area."

"He's awake?" she asked, focusing on the important part.

Christina nodded, her eyes welling with tears. "He has a concussion where some debris hit his head, but he's very lucky. No broken bones, only a few stitches. No internal damage."

"What happened?"

"He was at the mill when a bomb went off."

Avery quickly reached out to the wall, because she knew she was going down. Her knees hit the floor with a painful sting, but at least they stopped her descent.

"Oh, Avery, I'm sorry," Christina said, kneeling down, too. "I thought Jacob had told you."

Avery only managed to shake her head. "Not much," she murmured. Images of broken bones, surgeries and traction had raced through her brain while she'd waited. "He didn't give any details. Just that Luke had been hurt."

"Men." Christina helped her to her feet, then led her down the hallway with an arm around her waist, though Avery couldn't really tell who was supporting who. All too soon they breached the forbidden doors that Avery had stared at for so long. "I'm so sorry he left you guessing, Avery. I guess he was freaked out by it all, too."

"I bet."

"From what we can tell," Christina said as they walked, "he was at the accounting office doing some work during the night. As he left, he heard a truck on the loading dock, which wasn't supposed to be there during mandatory shutdown. He found the makings for a bomb in there—"

Oh, lord.

"Mark is involved somehow, too."

"Mark?"

Christina nodded. "The police are with them now."

"Mark made it out, too?" she asked as they came into a waiting room filled with Blackstones, including KC with little Carter, Nolen and Mary.

"Yes," Jacob said, reaching out to pull her close for a quick hug. "I'm so sorry. All I could think about was Luke."

"I understand."

"I was there while the police spoke with him,"

Jacob said. "Looks like Mark drove one of his parents' work vans into the mill loading dock, intending to blow it up with a bomb made from fertilizer. Luke found evidence of embezzlement on Mark's computer." Jacob shook his head. "Mark tied Luke to the truck and was gonna leave him there."

"Why?" Avery gasped.

Jacob took on a very uncomfortable look. The women glanced at each other. "Jacob, hon, you can tell us," Christina said.

KC appeared at his side. She looked at Avery in sympathy. "I'm sorry, Avery, but from Luke's account, it seems Mark was trying to marry you for money. He resented Luke's interference."

She rubbed up and down Jacob's back with her palm. "Mark called the Blackstones the golden sons. Said that they came back and took over everything he wanted. Said he'd ruin the whole town rather than let them take it."

Avery squeezed her eyes shut, unable to process it all. "What about the mill?"

"Zach is there now, assessing the damage," Jacob said. "But it's confined to the admin building, so fingers are crossed that it's minimal."

"Thank goodness," Christina said, echoing all their thoughts.

A doctor came into the room and called for their attention. Everyone turned. "Luke has asked to see his family, and I've granted permission, but only immediate family for now, please. He's not in serious danger, but I'd like to keep him overnight to observe him. The rest of you will get your chance soon enough."

Murmurs of relief spread through the room. There were hugs before the men gathered near the door. Aiden spoke quietly with Christina, who came and took Avery's hand, leading her down the hallway with the men. Avery's heart pounded. After all, she wasn't family.

"Christina, maybe I should go back," she whispered.

The other woman squeezed her hand. "Don't be silly."

Maybe Christina didn't know what had happened the last time she and Luke had seen each other. "Christina, really, this is a bad idea."

The men paused outside a door. Aiden turned to look at her. "No, Avery, it isn't. Luke needs you here, just as much as he needs us."

Only he didn't.

There was no time to explain as everyone moved inside. The beep of monitors made Avery wince. She'd been around many patients before who were hospital-bound in serious condition or in a coma. But this, this was different. This was Luke. Thoughts of him hurting and near death were almost her undoing.

He lay still on the bed, bandages around his head and one arm. Avery studied his body, looking for signs that would tell her about the damage, but couldn't find them. Her gaze traveling back up, and she found his amber eyes open and trained directly on her. Then his unhampered hand lifted, reaching out to her.

Despite what had happened between them, Avery couldn't stop herself from moving forward. She parted the crowd, resting with her hand in his, fir gers laid lightly against his wrist so she could feel that life-giving pulse for herself. Even so, she couldn't lift her eyes to his. Then he might see the utter devastation she'd been through over the past few hours. She blinked away the wash of tears. But she couldn't let go of that hand.

Not yet.

"Good to see ya, brother," Aiden said. Jacob murmured the same.

Luke let his bandaged head drop against the pillows with a wince. "Glad I'm still here to be seen."

Christina's tears were much freer than Avery's. She skirted around Jacob to give Luke a hug. "The doctor says everything will be okay?"

"Yep. There was absolutely no reason for them to med-flight me here. An ambulance would have been perfectly acceptable."

Jacob smirked. "Especially since Luke hates flying."

"Well, it did wake me up hella quick."

"I bet."

Avery could see Luke's hard swallow before he asked, "The mill?"

"Zach is there to evaluate the fire, last I spoke to him. If everything's sound, the plant floor and outbuildings will be saved with only smoke damage. The admin building wasn't so lucky. It will have to be rebuilt."

"I got electronic copies of the emails. Zach has the log-in info. Make sure the police check his home computer."

Aiden straightened, his height imposing. "Then we'll nail Mark's ass to the wall."

"He made it out?" Luke asked.

His heartbeat sped up beneath her fingertips.

Jacob nodded. "From what the police chief said, he had a spot all picked out to shelter in when the bomb went off, so he could claim it was an accident. Didn't work out so well for him."

Luke glanced around, then zeroed back in on his twin. "Why?"

Jacob looked to Aiden for confirmation before he said, "Part of the concrete wall came down on his legs."

Avery gasped, shocked, but found little sympathy in her heart. Mark had made his choice; he got what he deserved.

Christina laid her hand on Aiden's arm. "I think that's enough business for now, right, guys?"

Aiden covered her hand with his own. "She's right. I'm glad you're gonna be okay, Luke."

"Me, too," Jacob added. "This is one hospital too many, in my opinion."

"Mine, too," Luke agreed.

The others turned to the door, but Luke refused to let go of her hand.

Avery studied their clasped hands, unsure of what to do or say to avoid tears she wouldn't be able to stop.

"Thank you for coming," Luke said.

"I couldn't not come," Avery conceded.

Because it was the truth. No matter how Luke felt about her now, she wouldn't have been able to stay away, knowing he'd been hurt. She wanted to ask about his legs, his previous injuries, but she daren't open that can of worms.

"I appreciate that, Avery. Especially after the

way I treated you the last time we were together." He squeezed her hand. "I've been trying to find a way to apologize, to let you know I didn't believe those things I said, but I didn't know how. So I took the coward's way out and stayed away."

"If you didn't believe them, why did you say them?"

"Because I was angry. And, I think, because it gave me an excuse to dismiss your concerns without having to evaluate their merit." He kissed the back of her hand, drawing her tears closer to the surface. "I wanted you to support me, to agree with me whole-heartedly. When you didn't, I lashed out. I'm sorry."

Avery wished the apology meant more. Luke had almost died. She didn't want him to be sorry. She wanted him to say he loved her, that he would stay for her. But she couldn't ask him for that, wouldn't.

"Does it really matter?" she asked. The *yes* bloomed on his face, but he'd just been through a terrible experience. Two in a year. He was thinking about now. She was thinking about the future. She squeezed his hand. "I just don't think I can do this, Luke."

Now that she knew he would be okay, she had to find the strength to end this. "I love you, more than I ever thought I could, but my life is here. My home, my job, these people." Her throat closed, choking her for a moment. To her chagrin, a tear marched a single line down her face. "Your dreams are elsewhere. And I don't want to be the one who holds you back."

Luke lay against the pillow, exhaustion graying his face. She was a horrible person to do this now. But she simply couldn't support him through recovery, then watch him walk away from her.

"I'm so sorry, Avery. The other day I made a mistake."

"I did, too," she said with a sad smile. "But I can't say I'll ever be sorry."

She made it to the door, but she couldn't force herself to open it. Maybe deep down, a part of her still wished he would say he loved her. That she was worth not walking away from. But she knew that wasn't the answer in the long run, either. So she took a deep breath and put her hand on the doorknob.

"It really was fun, wasn't it?" she asked.

He nodded, his face grim.

She let herself out the door, down the hall and out to the parking lot. Her car provided the solitude she needed. She cried all the way back to her house. Only when wrapped tightly inside bedsheets that still smelled like Luke did she close her eyes, and let herself wish it was all a dream.

Luke finally spotted that unique combination of blonds in Avery's gorgeous hair at the far side of the ice rink at Rockefeller Center. He'd been searching for an hour in the crowds of New York City holiday visitors. The doorman at Aiden and Christina's New York apartment had been extremely helpful, since he'd recognized Luke and had helped Avery plan her route before she'd left today.

When Luke had finally returned home for the woman he couldn't live without, it had never occurred to him that he wouldn't just waltz into Avery's clinic

and sweep her off her feet. What an arrogant dumbass
he was.

Now he was hot on her trail, rueful and jealous.
He'd have loved to have traveled with her, but he'd
never told her that... He'd never told her a lot of
things.

How could she reciprocate when he'd offered her
nothing in the first place? Not even a phone call since
he'd left Black Hills. So she'd set out to find adventure on her own.

He'd resorted to begging his brother for info. The
connection between Luke and both his brothers had
strengthened in the past month. Though he and Jacob
had always been close, they were now never out of
touch for more than a day. He and Aiden texted a lot,
and called more often than they ever had.

Luke had missed them while he was in North Carolina, more than he'd thought he would. He'd gone
home to share his news, and was grateful that Christina had helped him find his little homebody in New
York City for the holidays. Now he only had to convince Avery to accept his humble Christmas gift.

She stood twenty feet from him, wrapped in a
thick suede jacket and wearing black gloves. But that
gorgeous hair was loose to the cold breeze in his favorite style. Not a hair band in sight.

As he angled toward her, he caught a glimpse of
her face. Her gaze jumped around as she took in the
people skating below her, then it moved up the giant
Christmas tree and across holiday decorations. She
seemed interested, happy, but not engaged in her surroundings.

An observer, not a participant.

Like she'd always been, from the first time he'd known her. Little Avery that watched everything from the sidelines. Never jumping in with both feet. Never forcing people to notice her. Never owning the excitement and life that were hers to enjoy.

Except for a short time…with him. He wanted to see that Avery again.

She'd turned in the other direction, so he navigated the crowd until he found a spot next to her and leaned against the rail. "Happy holidays, Avery."

Startled, she turned to him. He got to glimpse a few seconds of welcome, of excitement, before that beautiful face shut down, hiding her emotions behind a polite mask.

"Luke. I didn't expect to see you here."

"I didn't expect to see you here, either," he said. "I thought I'd find you in Black Hills, at the clinic."

A slight frown wrinkled her careful expression. "Why would you expect to see me anywhere?"

Because I can't imagine going through one more step of my life without you. Hmm…maybe a bit much. He should start slower.

"Because I couldn't imagine sharing my big news with anyone but you."

She nodded slowly. "The big meeting was this week?"

"It was." Luke had met with his racing sponsor. Avery's sad eyes told him she expected him to expound on the incredible deal he'd accepted. But… "After all the wining and dining he'd done, I don't think it went quite how he'd planned."

Avery took a slow breath in, exhaling a white puff of air after a moment too long. "What do you mean?"

"I told him I'd love to represent their company…
in two seasons. Not one."

Avery might have the calm bearing of a sphinx,
but he could tell he'd startled her. Still, she wasn't
jumping through his hoops very fast.

"What did he think about that?"

"Well, he was a little shocked." To say the least.
"But I had a few offers of my own up my sleeve."

He slipped a little closer, his heart speeding up just
from being near her. "I offered to shoot a comeback
movie chronicling my journey back to racing, at my
own expense, for them to use for promotional purposes. I'd already talked to Bobby Joe, who agreed
to stay on for an additional year."

Luke could read the shock in those beautiful blue
eyes, but he wasn't through yet. "All for a stake for
each of them in my new racing venture."

"You see—" Luke grinned, so at peace with his
decision that it seemed unreal "—I've arranged to
purchase that old racetrack outside of town. I'm cre-
ating a racing experience that allows people to experience driving a race car at a professional facility,
along with professional and amateur training. Jeff is
going to help me."

She shook her head. "Luke, you can't give up your
dream—"

"That is, when I'm not racing myself."

The mask dropped, giving him a glimpse of the
sheer misery she felt, but she remained silent.

"I managed to convince them I was worth the wait.
And that they should develop the whole me, not just
the racing me. So I win, they win and the town wins."

"Wow. That's awesome," she said. Her breath

shook a little. He could tell she truly was excited for him, not just saying the words, even though her eyes quickly darkened again.

"I figure it will be something I love, that I can do from home in my off-season. And it'll help bring more jobs and revenue to the town," he said. "And it's all because of you."

Those beautiful blues widened. "Me?"

"Yep. You and that hour back on the old track. I never would have thought of doing this if you hadn't planned something so special for me, Avery." To his surprise, his throat tried to close.

"I just— I knew that would be special for you."

Of course she had. Because she understood what he needed, even when he was being stubborn and stupid.

She glanced out over the skaters. "Your family will be thrilled that you'll be around more often."

Luke nodded, not quite trusting his voice. When he finally had his emotions under control, he said, "I hope you will be, too."

A look of sheer panic bloomed on her face and she started to shake her head, but Luke was having none of that.

"As you already know, I can be persistent when I want something really bad. And right now, I'm after something that I want more than anything I've had in my life."

Her voice was barely above a whisper. "What's that?"

"You."

She wasn't giving an inch. "What if I can't do this?"

"Then I'll be the saddest, loneliest man Black Hills has ever known."

Right there in front of God and country, he got down on his knee. Avery blushed, trying to pull him up, but he wasn't budging until she said yes.

"Avery, I love you." Reaching into his coat pocket, he pulled out something a little less traditional than an engagement ring. Instead, he'd had a custom key made, engraved with their names and the year. A key to something far more important than a car—no, this was a symbol for the commitment he had a hard time putting into words. But he had to try. "I've spent my entire life running, not realizing I was looking for a home. I found it—in you. Will you be there with me, every day, as I build a new life? Knowing I'm leaving the key to my heart with you, safe and sound?"

Seeing her excitement light her up was the greatest gift he'd ever been given. But her next words gave him pause.

"On one condition."

"What's that?"

"That you continue to drag me into all kinds of adventures. You know, someone told me once fun's the only thing that makes life worth living." She grinned big this time, letting the love he'd felt from her all along shine in her gaze. "After all, who better to show me how to have fun than Renegade Blackstone?"

Oh, yeah. "It's a deal."

* * * * *

*If you liked this novel, pick up these other
sexy Southern reads from Dani Wade*

*HIS BY DESIGN
A BRIDE'S TANGLED VOWS
THE BLACKSTONE HEIR*

All available now from Harlequin Desire!
***
*If you're on Twitter, tell us what you think
of Harlequin Desire! #harlequindesire*

REQUEST YOUR FREE BOOKS!
2 FREE NOVELS PLUS 2 FREE GIFTS!

HARLEQUIN®

Desire

ALWAYS POWERFUL, PASSIONATE AND PROVOCATIVE

YES! Please send me 2 FREE Harlequin® Desire novels and my 2 FREE gifts (gifts are worth about $10). After receiving them, if I don't wish to receive any more books, I can return the shipping statement marked "cancel." If I don't cancel, I will receive 6 brand-new novels every month and be billed just $4.55 per book in the U.S. or $5.24 per book in Canada. That's a savings of at least 13% off the cover price! It's quite a bargain! Shipping and handling is just 50¢ per book in the U.S. and 75¢ per book in Canada.* I understand that accepting the 2 free books and gifts places me under no obligation to buy anything. I can always return a shipment and cancel at any time. Even if I never buy another book, the two free books and gifts are mine to keep forever.

225/326 HDN GH2P

Name _____ (PLEASE PRINT) _____

Address _____ Apt. # _____

City _____ State/Prov. _____ Zip/Postal Code _____

Signature (if under 18, a parent or guardian must sign)

Mail to the **Reader Service**:
IN U.S.A.: P.O. Box 1867, Buffalo, NY 14240-1867
IN CANADA: P.O. Box 609, Fort Erie, Ontario L2A 5X3

Want to try two free books from another line?
Call 1-800-873-8635 or visit www.ReaderService.com.

* Terms and prices subject to change without notice. Prices do not include applicable taxes. Sales tax applicable in N.Y. Canadian residents will be charged applicable taxes. Offer not valid in Quebec. This offer is limited to one order per household. Not valid for current subscribers to Harlequin Desire books. All orders subject to credit approval. Credit or debit balances in a customer's account(s) may be offset by any other outstanding balance owed by or to the customer. Please allow 4 to 6 weeks for delivery. Offer available while quantities last.

Your Privacy—The Reader Service is committed to protecting your privacy. Our Privacy Policy is available online at www.ReaderService.com or upon request from the Reader Service.

We make a portion of our mailing list available to reputable third parties that offer products we believe may interest you. If you prefer that we not exchange your name with third parties, or if you wish to clarify or modify your communication preferences, please visit us at www.ReaderService.com/consumerchoice or write to us at Reader Service Preference Service, P.O. Box 9062, Buffalo, NY 14240-9062. Include your complete name and address.

HD15

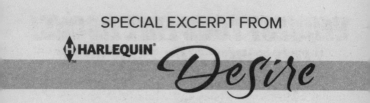
James Kavanagh liked working with his hands. Unlike his
eldest brother, Liam, who spent his days wearing an Italian
tailored suit, James was most comfortable in old jeans
and T-shirts. Truth be told, it was a good disguise. No one
expected a rich man to look like a guy who labored for a
paycheck.

That was fine with James. He didn't need people sucking
up to him because he was a Kavanagh. He wanted to be
judged on his own merits.

At the end of the day, a man was only as rich as his
reputation.

As he dipped his paintbrush into the can balanced on the
top of the ladder, he saw movement at the house next door.
Lila's house. A house he'd once known all too well.

It didn't matter. He was over her. Completely. The two of
them had been a fire that burned hot and bright, leaving only
ashes. It was for the best. Lila was too uptight, too driven,
too everything.

Still, something was going on. Lila's silver Subaru was parked in its usual spot. But it was far too early for her to be arriving home from work. He gave up the pretense of painting and watched as she got out of the car.

She was tall and curvy and had long blond curls that no amount of hair spray could tame. Lila had the body of a pinup girl and the brains of an accountant, a lethal combo. Then came his second clue that things were out of kilter. Lila was wearing jeans and a windbreaker. On a Monday.

He could have ignored all of that. Honestly, he was fine with the status quo. Lila had her job as vice president of the local bank, and James had the pleasure of dating women who were uncomplicated.

As he watched, Lila closed the driver's door and opened the door to the backseat. Leaning in, she gave him a tantalizing view of a nicely rounded ass. He'd always had a thing for butts. Lila's was first-class.

Suddenly, all thoughts of butts and sex and his long-ago love affair with his frustrating neighbor flew out the window. Because when Lila straightened, she was holding a baby.

Don't miss FOR BABY'S SAKE
by USA TODAY bestselling author Janice Maynard.
Available August 2016!

And meet all the Kavanagh brothers in the
KAVANAGHS OF SILVER GLEN series—
In the mountains of North Carolina, one family discovers
that wealth means nothing without love.

A NOT-SO-INNOCENT SEDUCTION
BABY FOR KEEPS
CHRISTMAS IN THE BILLIONAIRE'S BED
TWINS ON THE WAY
SECOND CHANCE WITH THE BILLIONAIRE
HOW TO SLEEP WITH THE BOSS
FOR BABY'S SAKE

www.Harlequin.com

Copyright © 2016 by Janice Maynard

Whatever You're Into… Passionate Reads

Looking for more passionate reads from Harlequin®?
Fear not! Harlequin® Presents, Harlequin® Desire and
Harlequin® Blaze offer you irresistible romance stories
featuring powerful heroes.

◆HARLEQUIN *Presents*

Do you want alpha males, decadent glamour and jet-set
lifestyles? Step into the sensational, sophisticated world of
Harlequin® Presents, where sinfully tempting heroes ignite a
fierce and wickedly irresistible passion!

◆HARLEQUIN *Desire*

Harlequin® Desire novels are powerful, passionate and
provocative contemporary romances set against a backdrop of
wealth, privilege and sweeping family saga. Alpha heroes with
a soft side meet strong-willed but vulnerable heroines amid a
dramatic world of divided loyalties, high-stakes conflict and
intense emotion.

◆HARLEQUIN *Blaze*

Harlequin® Blaze stories sizzle with strong heroines and
irresistible heroes playing the game of modern love and lust.
They're fun, sexy and always steamy.

Be sure to check out our full selection of books
within each series every month!

www.Harlequin.com

HARLEQUIN®

A *Romance* FOR EVERY MOOD™

Love the Harlequin book you just read?

Your opinion matters.

Review this book on your favorite book site, review site, blog or your own social media properties and share your opinion with other readers!